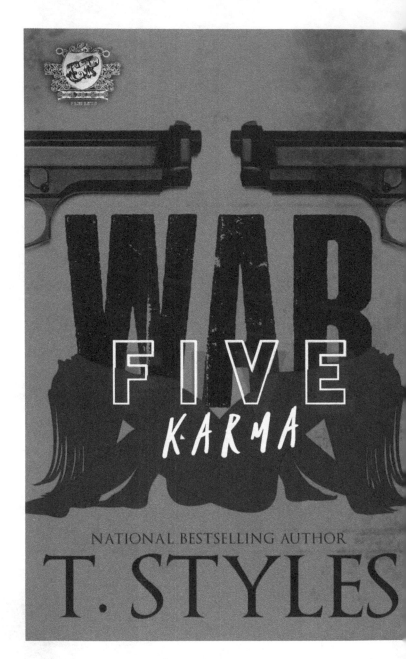

NATIONAL BESTSELLING AUTHOR

T. STYLES

ARE YOU ON OUR EMAIL LIST?

SIGN UP ON OUR WEBSITE

www.thecartelpublications.com

OR TEXT THE WORD: CARTELBOOKS

TO 22828

FOR PRIZES, CONTESTS, ETC.

CHECK OUT OTHER TITLES BY THE CARTEL PUBLICATIONS

WAR 5: KARMA

WWW.THECARTELPUBLICATIONS.COM

By T. STYLES   5

WAR 5:
KARMA
By
T. Styles

Library of Congress Control Number: 2019918155

ISBN 10: 1948373335

ISBN 13: 978-1948373333

Cover Design: Book Slut Girl

First Edition
Printed in the United States of America

What Up Fam,

This will be short and sweet. While I type this love note to you guys, I'm thinking of how fast I can get my thoughts down into this letter so that I can hurry up and get this book to you. On Movas, after I read *WAR 5*, I had to go pull T. out of her writing to just look at her in awe! If this book does not leave your mouth open, I'm not sure what else to tell you.

Ok, I'm gonna leave you with this, cherish yourselves and your love ones, especially during this holiday season. And I hope and pray that the new year brings you clarity and prosperity!

With that being said, keeping in line with tradition, we want to give respect to a vet or new trailblazer paving the way. In this novel, we would like to recognize:

ROBYN CRAWFORD

Robyn Crawford is a producer, creative director, author and former assistant to the late great Whitney Houston. Her novel, *A Song for You: My Life with Whitney Houston* is a personal and heartfelt memoir of how Robyn and Whitney met and became friends and navigated their friendship throughout Whitney's stellar career. After remaining silent for so many years, Robyn finally gets to share the Whitney Houston she knew and loves. Make sure you check it out!

Aight, I'm done. Enjoy yourselves with this one!

God Bless!

Charisse "C. Wash" Washington
Vice President
The Cartel Publications
www.thecartelpublications.com
www.facebook.com/publishercwash
Instagram: publishercwash
www.twitter.com/cartelbooks
www.facebook.com/cartelpublications
Follow us on Instagram: Cartelpublications
#CartelPublications
#UrbanFiction
#PrayForCece
#RobynCrawford

By T. STYLES

#War5

WAR 5: KARMA

PROLOGUE
THE PAST

*T*he fireplace crackled.

And slow music soothed the room as Banks and Bet set out to make another baby. She was lying on her back with him at her side, kissing her lips softly.

Delicately even.

This despite her body jerking up and downward, as Stretch, his most trusted soldier, and surrogate father to his other children, Spacey, Joey and Harris — sexed her hard. And since the plan had always been to have a large family, ten children to be exact, they were trying again.

When Stretch pressed deeper into her wetness, Bet's mouth opened as she experienced ecstasy. Of course, the arrangement was about giving Banks another child, but it was obvious that she was also enjoying herself a great deal, despite being in a missionary position.

Banks couldn't complain.

He wouldn't if he wanted to.

At the end of the day, he didn't care what was done to her body as long as his goal was met. It also didn't miss him that had this been Nikki, his first love, the situation may have been *different. He would've acted a bit irrational and maybe even jealous.*

"I'm sorry, boss." Stretch said as he looked at Banks with guilt. "I can't cum yet. It's, it's too hard." He wiped sweat from his brow as if he'd been lifting heavy weights.

Banks was annoyed. The last thing he needed was to be in bed with them for another thirty minutes. So, he rose and placed a hand on Stretch's shoulder as his dick was still nestled inside of her body. "Take all the time you need, just give me a son when you're done." He walked toward the door.

"Yes, yes, sir," he continued to move slowly to keep Bet warmed up. "I will...I will try to hurry."

"Good, I'm gonna get a drink." Banks said.

When he exited and closed the bedroom door, he heard the movements inside the bedroom getting more intense and passionate. He also heard Bet moaning like a whore. And again, he didn't care. Stretch could fuck her for five hours as long as it netted him another child.

When he made it to his barroom, he was surprised to see Jersey sitting by the fire. Her eyes were on the flames, as if she could read her future. For some reason, he took a moment to appreciate each detail of her body.

Something he hadn't done before.

Her hair was in a fussy bun on top of her head and soft strands hung at her shoulders. The glow from the crackling fire lit up her skin and the black spaghetti strap, connected to the top she wore gave up on one side, causing a slight exposure of her cleavage. Since she was also wearing yoga pants, he was able to catch every curve of her thighs.

When he found himself staring too hard, he walked inside. "Mason tapped out again?" He made himself a whiskey over rocks and poured her a fresh glass of Merlot. "Cause he was talking big shit earlier tonight."

"You know how he be after he eats." She accepted the drink, took a sip and pulled up her strap. "I can't blame him though. Your chef went all out today." Her eyes rolled from his eyes to his feet. "I can't understand why you not a big boy."

He sat next to her, but not too closely. "Nah, you gotta pace yourself."

"Pace yourself huh?"

"I'm serious. I eat a little and then I push back from the table. The same goes for my drink. Unlike your mans who go hard all the time." He chuckled.

"Oh, so he my man's now?"

He shrugged. "Well, your last name is Lou."

She giggled. *"You got me right there."* Another sip. *"And I knew he was gonna be sleep too. He a mess."* She sipped again.

"You just figuring that out?" He asked.

"Yep." She looked away and back at him. *"And you should've told me."* She pointed at herself right above the cleavage. *"You've known him way longer and I didn't get the memo."*

"I got you next time." He readjusted a little, as her eyes met his. *"Trust me."*

The conversation was frivolous and without meaning, but it allowed them the chance to get to know one another, although they were unsure why.

Fifteen minutes later...

"...so, I'm dancing right." She placed her wine glass on the table and stood in the middle of the floor. *"...so...so this lil dude comes up behind me, reaches between my legs and paws my pussy. Palm up so it's sitting in the middle of his hand. And I'm looking behind me like, I know this lil' boy not crazy. Except he was."*

Banks was laughing hysterically as he held his stomach. He wasn't one to get off his game by showing emotion, so it was refreshing to laugh so hard. The two shared similar moments in the past, but this seemed more authentic. As if they were connecting on another level.

"You laughing but I'm serious." She giggled, to the point of holding her stomach. "I didn't know what to do! I was too much in shock."

For some reason, the thought of a little boy-grabbing asses was hilarious to him. And then there was the thing with her body. As she performed the story, Banks couldn't help but notice that she was stacked in all the right places.

No cellulite.

Not a dent or dimple.

Sheer perfection.

"I'm sorry, but a kid going for his is not something I take lightly. He has a future in the confidence department." He sipped the rest of his drink and headed to the bar once more. "Want another?"

She quieted down and looked at him intensely. "You drinking with me?"

"Have I ever let you down?" He winked and made their drinks.

She smiled.

They both took their seats.

Followed by deep sips.

"You know, you don't have to do it the way you're doing it right?" She pointed at the door. "I mean, unless you...prefer it the natural way."

"What you talking about?"

"The baby thing. With Stretch and Bet."

He nodded and shifted a little in his seat. Why did she have to destroy the moment? "Mason told you? About who I am."

"He talks a lot when he's drunk." Banks stood up and she softly pulled his hand down to the sofa. "Please, please don't tell him about this. He'll kill me. And I'll never, ever let this get out."

Banks truthfully didn't care if she knew he was born female, since she was family, he just wished Mason could hold his secrets, especially when drinking. "Wow."

"I fake like I'm clueless about a lot of things around Mason. He likes it that way. But I'm aware." She sat back. "I just, I just wanted to say that you can have your egg removed and Stretch's sperm implanted. And that everything can be done in a doctor's office." She took another sip. "A friend of mine did that last year. Had a beautiful baby girl."

"I...I didn't think about that honestly." He shrugged, still fucked up about Mason letting out his life-long secret. "I keep *forgetting that technology has come a long way. I heard the chances of twins are higher that way though."*

"That's even better." She smiled. "Cause then you can have more than one." She shrugged. "I'm only suggesting it because, I mean, she is your wife."

He looked away.

Curious at his reaction, she leaned in to see him closer when she felt he didn't give a fuck. "You don't care, do you?" She placed her glass on the table. "It doesn't bother you that they have sex?"

He looked at her. The answer was all in his eyes.

Nah. He didn't.

"You, you don't love her?"

He sat back.

"Banks."

Silence.

She picked up her glass. "Okay." She sipped wine. "Answer me this, what do you care about? Who do you care about other than your kids? And Mason."

He looked deeper. "When I see it, I'll let you know."

She felt flushed.

She knew he wasn't talking about her, but the power in his voice made her feel as if he was.

"What you niggas up to now?" Mason said entering, wearing a white robe tied so tightly around the waist he resembled a snowman.

They separated a little although they remained close.

Mason walked up to the bar. "So ya'll just gonna ignore a nigga?"

"I'm kinda tired." She said. It was a lie, had he not walked in she could've stayed up all night.

"Have a drink with me first." Mason continued.

Banks rose. "Nah, man, I'm out." He drank the rest of his whiskey, placed a firm hand on Mason's shoulder and made his exit.

"Me too." She said kissing Mason on the cheek.

Mason grabbed her hand, roughly as usual. "You leaving me?"

"Kinda. I mean, the party is over. Shouldn't have slept on us."

Mason shrugged, made him a drink and flopped on the sofa.

CHAPTER ONE

The snow fell heavily on the Wales Estate in Maryland. The beautiful scene was reminiscent of the holidays, but today was all about business.

So much happened since Banks had been back in America. For months he hadn't seen Mason during this period until he popped up over his house earlier that day. The reason was simple, Mason fucked his wife on his island, tearing up their bond.

They were still meeting in his office, when Banks' maid indicated that someone was waiting outside the mansion.

Eager to see what was going on, they exited the office and made it to the foyer and then the front door. Joey, Spacey, Shay and Minnesota were already waiting, their gaze outside. But it was his youngest daughter Minnesota who shocked him because he could've sworn, he saw the handle of a gun on her waistline.

And then there was the expression on her face. It was one that he hadn't seen before. Did the troubles on Wales Island change her that much? She appeared regal, strong and powerful. Something like Nidia and her stance shocked him to the core.

Remembering the strangers in front of the home, he walked past his spawn, with Mason at his side. He didn't bother telling his children to go to their rooms; they'd already been exposed to life in all its most violent forms on the island.

It was time to deal with the situation at hand.

Besides, winter was here.

Looking outside and past the heavy snow which turned everything white, he saw a sea of men dressed in fine coats, standing in front of BMW trucks. In protection mode, the Wales clan moved behind their father eager to defend him with their lives.

From where he stood, he could see a Latino man, flanked by two armed men. When they saw Banks exit the mansion, the strangers walked toward the house. One man was holding a red umbrella over another's head and Banks could tell immediately that he was the boss.

"Dad, I saw him on the island," Joey whispered. "When you were gone."

Banks nodded as the Latino man approached, a mechanical grin covered the stranger's face. "My name is Mr. Bolero and I represent the man who helped you and the Nunez family on Skull Island." He said with a heavy accent.

Banks frowned, as snow fell harder. "Skull Island?"

He laughed. "Mr. Wales, before you buy property you should know the history. Unfortunately for you, you failed to do the work and now you owe."

"But I gave them the land," Banks said.

"Exactly, so why you here?" Mason added as if he were talking to him.

Bolero stared with intensity at them both. "Does the land mean to get rid of the point that my boss lost two daughters? Emetine and Oswalda Nunez."

Now Banks was definitely confused. One thing in his mind had nothing to do with the other.

"What do you want?"

Mr. Bolero clapped his hands once. "To bring understanding. It is the reason I'm here." He raised his hand, all five fingers pointed to Banks' door. "Shall we begin?"

THE LIVING ROOM – WALES MANSION

Mr. Bolero sat in a recliner across from Mason, Shay, Spacey and Joey who were propped up on the sofa. Minnesota was standing near her father, behind him as if watching his back. In all honesty, she was fulfilling her duties accurately. After all, she was strapped.

Mr. Bolero was also with soldiers, including Tobias Nunez, who Banks had a history with on Wales Island.

As the room remained silent, the maid brought Mr. Bolero his requested coffee. He greedily sipped loudly, until the cup was empty, despite the liquid being scalding hot. When he was done, he wiped his mouth with the back of his hand and burped. He wasn't being rude, instead he had a tendency to be, well, tacky.

"I 'on't mean no harm but you wanna tell us why you here?" Spacey asked. "Because I know I speak for my father too when I say we confused."

"You a Louisville?" Mr. Bolero asked.

"Nah. I'm a Wales." His tone was proud and laced with honor.

Mr. Bolero clapped his hands together. "Okay, well let me be frank. I work for a man whose name will remain nameless."

"Why?" Mason asked.

"Because, with all due respect, I don't fucking trust you." He looked at each of their faces. "Any of you for that matter."

"So, you come to our home and don't give us enough info to make a decision on if we should even be dealing with you?" Spacey continued. "What kind of sense does that shit make?"

Normally it was Mason who would disrespect. However, that was before he heard Mr. Bolero's name. But now since he smelled coke money in the air, it was he who fell back while Spacey took full reign.

"You're correct. I am in your home so allow me to give you some information you can use." He sat up. "You purchased my boss's property. So—"

"Like I said, we gave it back," Banks interrupted. "So why are you here?"

Mr. Bolero shuffled a little in his seat. "True. You gave it back. But, before doing so, two of my boss's children were murdered. Now he's deeply hurt about this. And where he's being kept, well, let's just say, they could care less about his feelings. That means he has to turn his attentions elsewhere."

"What that got to do with us?" Minnesota interrupted.

"Nothing at this point in the scenario. Although I will say this, my client is forced to grieve alone. You have no idea what it feels like to lose a child. Two at that!"

Banks glared. He had lost Harris and as of the moment, he never fully grieved. There was too much to be done and so little time. So yes, he understood what it meant to lose a child.

"What about Ives Nunez?" Banks said. "I thought they were his children." Banks may have remained quiet mostly, but it was with reason. He was thinking, learning and assessing the stranger's every word and move.

"Ives is a joke. And since you've met the man and been in his company, I know you will agree." He looked at Tobias. "What do they call a person who acts as a stand in for a real relationship?"

"A beard." Tobias responded, also with an accent.

Mr. Bolero clapped his hands once. "Yes, yes, a beard."

"Let's keep shit real. Where the fucking coke?" Mason asked. "Because I know that's why you're here."

Banks glared his way. He loved the man but once again he never knew when to be silent.

Mr. Bolero laughed like Santa Claus on Christmas day. "Unfortunately, I don't carry it on me but you're right, my boss's proposal involves a lot of it." He shrugged. "And a lot of money too. But let's be clear, you owe. And as a result, you will work off your debt, until he's paid in full."

"What if we don't?" Banks asked.

"I don't like threatening people but let's just say you have a lot to lose." He looked at the Wales offspring and Banks caught the hint, evident by the thump in his heart.

Spacey, Joey, Shay and Minnesota's hands hovered over their hips and it was at that time that Banks realized they *all* were packing. After leaving Wales Island, no one felt comfortable without a clapper and so they thought it best to be ready at all times.

Upon seeing the *cowboy gun hover*, Mr. Bolero's men grabbed their weapons and Banks raised his hand when his children aimed barrels in response. "Settle down!" Banks looked at his children. "It's okay." The Wales clan continued to stay on the ready, deciding to ignore their father's request. "Put 'em the fuck away!" He yelled louder. "Now!"

Slowly they tucked their weapons back against their hip lines and Mr. Bolero's men did the same.

"Now that we all know we're ready for battle, here are my terms." Mr. Bolero rubbed his hands together. "I will supply your needs. And as a result, you are to move the product we provide. *Exclusively*. When done, all money is to be brought to me. For which you will be paid a generous stipend."

"So, your boss has a price for his dead children?" Banks said. "I mean, their deaths have a weight in coke?" He glared.

"This is not a negotiation. These are my terms and you will honor them too or die."

He reached into his pocket and handed Banks a piece of paper. "This has to be almost eight thousand keys."

"It's ten."

Banks felt dizzy while Mason felt as if he officially hit the jackpot.

Banks readjusted. "There is no way we can—."

"You don't and you die." Mr. Bolero shrugged. His need to be polite went out the window. "Your choice." He rose. "I'm leaving Tobias here. To watch over our investment. And since he already has a relationship with your family, I trust his presence will go smoothly."

Minnesota smiled and then cleared it quickly. "Your boss trusts us with another one of his spawn?"

"Tobias can take care of himself just fine. And you of all people should know it."

She shuffled and crossed her arms over her chest.

"I don't allow coke into my house." Banks said, still stewing over the forced relationship. "Don't bring it here."

"Where you store the product is up to you. As long as it's safe. Because let me be clear, there will be no excuses for lost packages. We will get our money." He walked toward the exit. "Enjoy the weather. I think the forecast is cocaine."

CHAPTER TWO

A light snowfall floated down to earth blessing everything on the ground with its presence. Windshield wipers working overtime, Banks was driving in his money green BMW talking to Jersey on the car phone. After his mother died during the winter, Banks despised the holiday season, but lately his opinion changed.

He was suddenly in the mood.

And he had Mrs. Claus to thank.

"...you said that the last time," she giggled. "I'm starting to believe you don't know what good food is because...I mean..."

"What you trying to say?" He hit a left on the road as smoothly as butter.

"What I'm trying to say?" She repeated. "Everything was gross!"

He chuckled. "Oh, so you playing right? Cause I know you not 'bout to act like you didn't crush the whole steak."

"I didn't." She giggled heavily causing him to smile. "And like I said, you don't have good taste."

"That's fucked up because I thought that pussy was sweet last night. But since I don't have good taste…"

She chuckled harder and he smiled again. Her laughter was always so light and cute, the epitome of femininity. "Ewwwww, you being gross, Banks."

He laughed and made a right. "Naw…I'm being real."

A deep breath. "Then how come it took days to see you?"

"I know."

"I'm serious, Banks. I be missing you. I want to see you more."

"I don't have to see you for you to know how I feel."

"So, what we doing then?" She continued. "About us?"

"Jersey." He paused. "Remember what I said. Let's keep it light. No pressure. You know that works best for me."

"But you—."

"What we have is good." He cut her off. "Stop trying to push the details."

"You're right. I don't want to be like her."

"It's not about Bet." He turned the heat on. "I'm a man of few words. But just know I haven't felt like this, ever. That's gonna have to be enough for right now."

"Whoa. I finally got an emotion out of the great Banks Wales."

"There you go again."

"I'm serious." She giggled. "I like it though."

"You always on your shit." He made a right.

"I'm falling, Banks. In love."

"I know you are." Was all he could say.

He continued down the road, although he missed his stop again upon hearing her words. He was feeling her too. That much was evident. But love was a different monster. However, considering the risk he was taking by simply talking to her, it was obvious that she was on his mind.

Still, Banks didn't do one single thing on a whim. Everything had to be thought out in advance, including his relationships. It was how he kept a peace of mind. But Jersey wanted everything now.

"One more question, what we gonna do?" She continued. "About Mason."

"I don't know." The moment she mentioned his name, he missed his turn again and bucked a U.

"Banks, we need to think about him eventually."

"Jersey." He wiped a hand down his face, leaned back further and maneuvered the wheel with his right.

"I can't do that right now. And it ain't cause I don't think it's important. It's just that—."

"I get it."

"He's a part of my history. My brother. And regardless of what he did to me, I fuck with him. Still."

"He wants to have sex with me."

"Don't let him." Banks glared. "We talked about that already too. All that will do is lead him on."

"I'm trying."

"He'll—."

WHAM.

Suddenly Banks' car was slammed from the right throwing his conversation off guard. "What the fuck!"

"Are you okay?" Jersey yelled, after hearing the noise.

When the car stopped Banks said, "I'ma hit you back." He pulled the glove compartment open, grabbed his loaded hammer and exited his vehicle to investigate. When he saw Bet's candy apple red Benz truck smoking, he glared.

Tucking his gun into his waistline, he rushed and snatched her door open. "Fuck is wrong with you?"

She stormed out, wearing jeans and a red leather jacket too small for the brutal weather. "You won't talk to me!" She tossed her arms up, almost hitting his face. "That's what's fucking wrong."

"Talk to you about what? We divorced! It's been over."

"But...I can't...I can't...please don't do this to me." She placed a hand over her heart. "Please don't do this to our family."

"I'm good with my family. It's you I cancelled."

This sent her on a whole 'nother level of rage. "You don't get to write me off!" She sniffled and wiped her tears with the back of her hand. The frigid air caused the tip of her nose to redden. "I'm your wife."

He held the sides of his face, not believing the madness. "You fucked my best friend. You anything but a wife. Not to me anyway."

"I apologized, Banks." She said softly. "It meant nothing. But how come you take Mason back, but divorce the person who...who been by your side? Who gave you children? It's not fair!"

"You went against our vows."

"So, if you're without sin then you can judge." She stepped closer. "So, tell me, Banks, are you in a position to judge me?"

He wasn't and for the first time, he didn't care. Throughout his life, the people he held close did what they wanted. Said what they wanted. Leaving him to pick up the pieces. He was tired of being a good guy.

He saw a quote somewhere that said, *You either die a hero, or live long enough to see yourself become a villain.* And he was moving in that direction.

"You scorned."

"You think I'm scorned? Are you crazy? I'm ready to kill!"

It was useless talking to her. Banks grabbed his phone and sent a text. When he was done, he looked at the damage on his car. The side of his vehicle was crushed but drivable and her front bumper was hanging off.

He grabbed her arm. "Listen, I want you to stay the fuck away from me." He pulled her closer. "Do you hear me? What you and I had is over."

"Never." She cried harder. "You are my whole world. My everything. And without you I will die. Is that what you want? To kill me."

"You should've thought about that before you took dick."

She sniffled. "You will pay for what you're doing." She promised. "I may have my faults, but I love you. And you ripping me apart."

He texted a few more times while ignoring her all together.

The fact that he was so carefree on his phone drove her insane. "You hate me, don't you?"

"Nah." He said.

She smiled. There was hope!

"I despise you." He explained.

Seconds later, Spacey pulled up in a red BMW truck and rushed up to them. When Bet saw her son, she was livid. "No, no, no! Why did you call him?"

Spacey quickly approached and touched his mother's arm. "Ma, what you doing?"

"You trying to turn my kids against me." She spit at Banks' feet. "It ain't enough for you to leave me. You want them to think bad about me too."

Banks walked toward his car.

"Don't walk away from me!" She yelled at his back.

"Ma!" Spacey grabbed her arm. "Stop it!"

The snow fell harder and she was so heated, the particles could barely stay on her face without melting away. "Let me talk to him!" She yelled at Spacey. "He's my husband! Please!"

Banks climbed in his car. "Take her home, son!"

"I'm going to go away forever!" She cried. "And then you'll be sorry, Banks! Because you won't be able to find me!"

"Get her out of here, Spacey." He repeated.

Since Banks appeared to be Teflon and hurt her feelings even more, she decided to cut deeper. "I can't believe you convinced me to fuck with you. I had no business sleeping with another bitch."

Banks smirked. "And you still crying over this plastic dick too. Fuck up out my face." He pulled off.

Bet dropped to her knees and cried as Spacey held her in his arms.

Spacey was parked in front of Bet's luxury apartment building in downtown Baltimore, while talking on the cell phone. The snow continued to trickle down to earth, covering the windows as Bet sat in the passenger seat of his truck crying.

When he ended the call, he tucked the phone back into his pocket and took a deep breath. "The tow company gonna pick your truck up later."

She nodded. "Thank you."

"Ma, the way you moving ain't it."

She wiped her tears and looked at the icy window. "I know."

"So why you doing shit like this? If you wanna get Pops back, insulting him an hitting up his car gonna push you further away from your goal."

She turned her body so that she could see his face. The pain in her eyes had his heart skipping beats. "I pray you never know what it feels like, to love hard and not have it returned. I pray you never have to wake up and feel like what's the point in living if you already dead."

"Ma, please don't talk like that."

"If I don't get him back..." she sniffled and wiped her nose with the back of her hand. "I need somebody to put me outta my misery. Can you do it, son? Please."

CHAPTER THREE

Snowflakes danced on the hairs of Mason, Derrick and Patterson's fur coats, as they walked toward an office building. The day lent itself to coke business, but the moment was all about bonding with his sons.

"So, I was like, bitch if you want this dick you better act like it," Patterson bragged. "And she was all—."

"First off, stop lying," Derrick interrupted, digging his hands deeper into his white coat to gather warmth. "You stay popping off 'bout some bitch you 'bout to fuck when we ain't seen none of 'em."

"How you sound?"

"Where are these females, huh? Tell me that. I ain't seen a one in the house."

Mason laughed as Patterson opened the door, allowing Mason to enter as Derrick followed. "He got a point." Mason chuckled. "Seeing is believing."

"As a matter of fact, if you introduced her to me, I bet I can pull her from you." Derrick bragged. "That's if she's real."

"Nigga."

"Serious. When I'm done, she'd act like you were never born."

They ascended the stairs. "And I bet I beat your ass too."

Mason stopped and glared upon hearing the words, grabbing Patterson's arm. They were playing at first but now things felt serious. "No, you won't. Because any bitch that would come between you and your brother ain't worth the time." His eyes were penetrating. "Do you hear me?"

"Yeah, I got it." Patterson said.

Mason released him.

Patterson was heated as he looked at Derrick. "Now you got Pops all mad and shit. That's why I can't tell you nothing."

"Ain't nobody — ."

RING. RING.

Mason removed his cell phone from his coat and frowned at the number on display. "Go 'head without me. I'll be up after this call." They nodded and bopped up the steps. Mason answered, "What, Howard?"

"I was calling to see if I could come over later." He paused. "I mean, that's if you not too busy."

"Will your mother be home?"

"No, I was coming to chill with you."

Mason dragged a hand down his face. "I already done told you we don't have shit to discuss. The relationship you have with her still breathes. Let that give you peace at night."

He hung up.

Ever since Mason saw his son raping Spacey on Wales Island, he pushed him away. Mainly because he felt bad for the Wales' spawn, but also himself. It wasn't enough that Spacey and Mason decided to keep the secret away from Banks. Mason knew if he ever found out he would be devastated, and their relationship would get nudged back even further. And at the end of the day, there was no relationship more important to Mason than the one he held with Banks. As a result, he would protect it at all costs.

"Aye, Pops, niggas is waiting!" Patterson yelled from the hallway. "What you gonna do?"

The boardroom inside the office building had chairs, but twenty-six of Mason's men stood around in coats, waiting on the word. Since the heat was off, because

Mason gave a few bucks to the janitor to let them use the space for business, provided they don't use the heating system, every time anyone breathed a fog cloud would pump from their nostrils.

When Mason walked inside, they all shifted a little in anticipation. After all, what was the reason for the meeting? They all knew that without Nidia's distribution channels, the streets were dry, so they were certain he was cutting them off for good. And not a man present wanted it to be true.

"We got work," Mason said plainly, stuffing his hands into his black fur coat.

All of his men gasped excitedly.

Amos, who had been with Mason for a while, and was the only surviving lieutenant after Banks took out Mason's whole crew at the beginning of the war, stepped up. "I thought the channels were closed. I mean, you getting work from Banks?"

Every man paused.

"Yeah. I am."

The way their bodies dipped, and their faces pinched together made it obvious they didn't approve.

"We dropped the beef in the name of getting money." Mason continued. "Be glad. It's Christmas, my niggas!"

"This dude took out everybody in our squad, Mason," Amos reminded him. "And you trust him enough to work for him again? No disrespect but this move sounds crazy, boss. And I ain't feeling it."

"Yeah, this feels disloyal...like to Brewer and Leonard who Banks murked during this shit." Marcus added. "You sure this the only way?"

"Not to mention he's a she." Lady Jay said crossing her arms over her chest. She was the epitome of femininity and didn't understand why Banks wanted to be anything other than what he was born to be.

A woman.

"I don't know about all that. I got my reasons for not fucking with Banks," Amos said pointing at her. "And I don't give a fuck about him being born a lady bitch." He focused back on Mason. "This all about him trying to kill me by having some niggas hide under the bed while I was fucking a female."

Lady Jay rolled her eyes. She may have garnered a little animosity by being one of the highest earners amongst Mason's squad, but there was no mistaking that the pretty young thing held her own.

"Listen, Banks is my guy, period," Mason said with all seriousness. "Name a war that didn't lose soldiers and I'll put a mill in every nigga's pocket in this room."

Silence.

"At the end of the day, we just made a coke deal big enough to set you up for life. And then your children's, children's lives. And you can take advantage of Banks' grace or step the fuck off. Your choice."

A few grunted but all knew they weren't going nowhere.

"So how you know you can trust him?" Amos continued. "How you know he won't run off again to a different island?"

"That's true, because every hitta in this room knows he wants out," Lady Jay continued. "And to be honest, I can't have my mind fucked with no more."

"I know because he ain't got no choice this time." Mason said. "Pumping coke is a do or die situation now. And you can't get better odds than that."

CHAPTER FOUR

S now mounds which turned to hard white icebergs were nestled in various corners around Maryland.

Mason, Derrick and Patterson rushed across town, in Baltimore County, to meet up with Banks as he said the matter was urgent. He called the meeting the day before, and Mason was sure it would be about the distribution process which he was eager to get started on. But when they made it to the parking lot of an abandoned building, they were surprised to see a gold and black 2018 Renegade Ikon coach motorhome waiting. It was surrounded by recognizable Wales soldiers.

"What the fuck?" Patterson said as he removed his red and green Gucci knit hat and scratched his head before putting it back on. "I thought we were going in the building."

"Let's just go inside and see what's up." Mason said as they piled out of the Mercedes truck. Readjusting the collar of his black fur coat, he repositioned his gold chain so that it hung perfectly as he bopped.

He desired to be on shine at all times.

After knocking in code, when Preach let them inside, they were taken aback at how luxurious Banks' motorhome was. Everything was outlined in wood and gold and it was extremely spacious.

Wales style.

Inside were Banks, Spacey, Joey, Minnesota, Shay and Tobias, all dipped in leather or fur coats. But it was white boy Trey and his best friend Ramirez that shocked Mason. Because everyone on the streets knew they dealt in opioids, a line of work Banks swore he would never venture into.

"What they doing here?" Derrick whispered to Mason.

"I don't know," he frowned. "You saw I just got here too."

Banks approached Mason with a smile. He was wearing a black leather coat, and lightly tinted shades which concealed his eyes. Everybody in the room looked and smelled like millions.

"You late." Banks shook his hand.

"What's going on?" Mason asked, looking around him at Trey and Ramirez, who were engaged in conversation and didn't appear to notice the Lou's. "Why we dealing with them dudes?"

"I got good news," Banks said, placing a hand on his back. "Come with me and I'll tell you everything you need to know."

The Lou's followed him deeper into the motorhome as Banks walked into the middle of the room. "Now since everyone's here, let's get started."

The Lou's pulled even closer.

All eyes on the king.

"With the situation I'm in, I found myself with more product than I can pump."

"Says who?" Mason said under his breath, mostly to be heard by his sons.

"So, I decided to solicit the help of my man right here." Banks shook White Boy Trey's hand. "This business venture will work out for everyone."

"Banks, you already know what it is." Trey said. "Your name is money on the streets and this deal is perfect for us. We have a coke market opening on the west coast so thanks for even looking our way."

"And my name not money on the streets?" Mason asked.

"Nah." He said honestly. "It's not."

"Nigga, I'll—."

Banks stopped his best with a palm to the center of his chest. "Listen to the plan." He gave him an intense look, warning him to fall back. "This deal is perfect. We give them our product and they give us the pills at a lower rate. Since their coke market ain't out here, that'll stop Nidia from—."

"Why though?" Mason shrugged repeatedly. "We dope boys. We ain't doctors. Fuck we gonna do with Vicodin?" He looked at Trey. "Let this Caucasian ass nigga handle that shit."

"You forgot who my mother is?" Banks asked Mason.

The room grew tense and it was obvious that Mason was looking for a reason to pop off. The goon simply wanted a war.

"Everybody calm down," Spacey said.

"Banks, this ain't us." Trey said. "I thought you already briefed your man on our deal. We just—"

"I can move this coke, Banks you know that." Mason said, cutting Trey off. "Ain't no need to jump ship when I got this. I got us! I'm already setting it up as we speak."

"Not without heat from Nidia. Trust me, if we move coke in her market she will be at our heads."

"She at our heads regardless." Mason said.

"True, but ain't no need in making shit worse by stepping on her toes. So, the focus is on getting money.

We can do that with Trey's package if we give him Bolero's coke."

"I'm not feeling moving no pills," Mason continued. "You not hearing me."

"Banks, no disrespect, but like I said I thought you talked to dude already." Trey said.

"Dude got a name." Mason said through clenched teeth.

"Oh, we know who you are." Ram said, in a Mexican accent so thick it was almost difficult to understand. "And we ain't got no respect for you either."

Mason grabbed the gun from his waist. "What, nigga?"

And just like that, the Lou clan released their weapons while Trey, Ram and their men removed theirs. Falling in suit with the Lou's, Spacey, Joey, Minnesota, Shay and Tobias also aimed at Trey and Ram.

Banks was irritated that once again Mason messed up his plans. But if a war popped off, he was already drafted on his best friend's side. "The meeting's over," Banks said to Trey and Ram as he removed his glasses. "Get out."

Trey glared. "My pleasure." He, Ram and their men walked toward the exit, everyone still aimed in their direction.

When they were gone Banks dropped his glasses on the counter and went ape. "Fuck is wrong with you, nigga?"

"Me?" Mason pointed at his self. "You 'bout to give our coke away to the first west coast nigga with a purse. Without even giving me a chance to do my work. That shit belongs to us!"

"First off, it ain't *ours*. Bolero bounding me to this shit." He beat his chest with a fist. "At any point you can walk away, and it'll still be on my head."

"But I wouldn't do that. You know that shit!"

"That ain't the fucking point!"

"Unc, we still feel as though you wrong." Patterson said. "You could've gave Pops a heads up about this meeting."

"Lil, nigga, when I'm talking business don't address me." Banks said pointing at him. "You out your pay grade."

"Okay, everybody bounce." Minnesota said. "Let them talk alone."

Patterson laughed at her. "I'm staying right—."

Minnesota fired into the ceiling, destroying her father's property.

Patterson and Derrick flinched.

"Let's go! Now!" Minnesota repeated.

Banks shook his head as it became more evident that she was ready for anything. When their spawn was gone Mason walked up to him. "I know you mad."

"It ain't about being mad. If you had a problem, we could've talked about it on the side. You don't go against me like that in public, ever!"

Mason knew he was speaking facts but when he was in rage mode, it was hard to stop him. He operated by an *act now and worry later* policy. "I'm sorry, man. I just...I mean, why don't you want to move the work? This shit goes down right, we can be, do, have anything we want."

"I can have anything I want now. What I need is my people safe. That means you too."

"You can have *anything* you want?" Mason repeated. "Because I can't." He looked into his eyes seriously.

Banks didn't know what he meant but thought it best to leave matters alone. "I told you we have to be smart with Nidia."

"And I'm saying she beefing with you no matter what. You know that. You selling pills just to stop the heat she bringing won't work." He stepped closer.

"What are you saying, Mason?"

"I'm saying that you always coming up with a plan that sometimes you forget to let shit be. Let's have fun."

Banks frowned. "Fuck is you talking about? Moving dope ain't fun."

"It used to be. When we first got started." Mason smiled and nudged his arm a little. Banks backed away. "Come on, man, you ain't even gotta touch Bolero's shit. I got everything. All you gotta do is give me one month to show you why the dope game is life. After that you can do whatever. No strings attached. That's my word."

CHAPTER FIVE

The blinds were open inside of Howard's luxury apartment, providing a spectacular view over the inner harbor. "Ma, I don't need all this meat," Howard said as he watched her stuff the deep freezer in his new home in downtown Baltimore. "I don't even cook that much." He scratched his recently shaped up mane and crossed his arms over his chest.

She placed the last pack of premium beef inside and closed the lid. "If you want me to cook, I can come over and make you meals for the week. That way you can always have something prepared and all you have to do is—."

"Nah, ma," he smiled, dropping his arms. "I'm good." He kissed her cheek. "Really." Although so much happened in their lives, he couldn't get over how expensive she looked. Even at the moment, her hair was curled to perfection, draping over her shoulders as if snow was not a problem. Even the 5 karat gold earrings in her ears blinged.

She placed a warm hand on the side of his face. "How come I don't believe you?"

"Come on. Stop it." He shuffled a little under her gaze. "Do you, do you ever think about Arlyndo?"

"My God, all the time," she said softly. "Which is why I have to know why you here, Howard? We have plenty space at the new house. I don't understand. Are you and your father that much at odds where you can't share the same mansion?"

His gaze fell downward, unable to hold his mother's eye contact. He couldn't tell her of all the evil things he'd done. He couldn't tell her that he was bisexual, with violent tendencies. But most of all he couldn't let her know that he'd been caught by Mason, raping Spacey.

"I'm just grown now." He joked. "Ain't a whole lot to it. It was time for me to leave the nest."

She gripped his face in both of her hands. "I don't know what's going on, but I want you to know I love you."

"I know you do."

When she grabbed her LV purse and walked toward the door, before leaving she looked back. "No matter what happens between you and your father, I'm here. Always."

He nodded and leaned against the wall.

When she left, his nose caught a whiff of the trashcan, which stunk to high heaven because he hadn't taken it out in days. When he walked out to dump the bucket, he stopped when he ran into Bet coming into her apartment.

They lived on the same floor.

Her hair was moist due to being snowed on and her eyes were bloodshot red. "You aight?" He asked. "You look like you been fighting."

She wiped her yellow face roughly and stuffed her hands into her jacket. "I'm fine." She shrugged. "I guess."

"You sure?"

"What are you, what are you about to do?" She stuttered. "Don't wanna be alone and could use the company."

"Taking my trash out." He looked toward the elevator. "I mean, uh, come with me."

She nodded repeatedly as if he'd asked her a question. And at the same time, he understood the look of confusion that sat on her face. He was confused about many things lately too.

"Thank you."

Entering the elevator, they were taken to the lowest level of the building. Both walked in silence, neither feeling much like talking. They continued to the dumpster in the same manner, but he was suddenly uneasy. Since his father wasn't speaking to him, he wasn't sure who knew about what he'd done to Spacey. At the end of the day, he needed to be cautious because for all he knew, she could shank him at any moment.

"So, what's up, Mrs. Wales?"

"Do me a favor."

"Anything."

"Don't call me Mrs. Wales again." She watched him dump his trash and sighed deeply. "Howard, physically, is there anything wrong with me?" She looked up at him with the eyes of a child, begging for approval. "Am I still attractive?"

She was.

"Yeah, I mean you look 'aight to me. Why you asking?"

"Banks is done with me." She threw her hands up. "I did everything for him, and this is how he treats me? Like I never mattered. Like I never existed. I mean, what kind of shit is that?"

"Maybe it's a good thing. Especially if ya'll been having problems for a while."

"How is this a good thing when my entire life has been that man? That everything I know, everything I am revolves around him."

He chuckled once. "Even after all of this time you still see her as a he?"

She looked at him seriously. "You've known Banks all of your life. Do you see him as anything different?"

He didn't.

She moved to the elevator with him walking closely behind her. When they were on the tenth floor, they dipped back to his place, all while she went on about Banks Wales and his travels.

It was getting kind of boring.

Sitting on the sofa, she finally grew quiet. It was as if she were replaying in her mind all their best and worst moments as a married couple. Still, she couldn't find relief.

He could see the weakness in her eyes, and it made his dick hard. "What do you want from me, Mrs. Wales?"

"I told you to stop calling me that." She removed her jacket and placed it on the arm of the sofa. It hit the floor. "I mean it."

"Well, what do you want from me, Bet? Right here. Right now."

She shrugged. "I don't know. Maybe, maybe a shoulder to cry on."

"Is that it?" He grabbed his dick, disrespectful like.

Silence.

She was weak and he decided to take charge. "Get over here." He zipped down his pants.

She glared. "What…what are you doing? I'm like a mother to you. I know you don't expect me to—"

"You ain't my mother. Stop playing games and get over here."

"Howard, please stop acting juvenile."

"The more time you waste, the less time we have to be together. Don't make me ask again. Let me take away some of your pressure."

Needing to feel something outside of pain, she pushed down her pants and panties and moved toward him naked from the waist down. Placing her hands on the edge of the sofa, she turned around preparing to take the dick.

He stopped her as he stroked himself. "Get it wet first."

"What?"

"On your knees. Lips open. Mouth wet."

She turned around and slowly fell to her knees. She breathed the dough smell of his dick and sucked him softly at first. His body tensed up just from the act. He couldn't believe that Banks' ex-wife and Spacey's mother was pleasuring him.

In his mind, it was something like poetic justice laced with a little revenge.

When he felt himself about to bust, he was about to tell her to rise so he could push into her, but she could feel the pulsating vein against her tongue and beat him to it.

Standing up quickly, she bent over and placed one hand on the sofa. The other she used to guide his dick into her wet pussy. Loving it rough, he yanked her hair and pulled backwards, before biting on her neck to the point of drawing a little blood.

"Look at you taking this dick," he said, feeling his body heating up.

"Shut up and fuck this pussy," she demanded. "Fuck it real good."

"What you think I'm doing, huh?" He bit his bottom lip and continued to bang into her body. "Huh, bitch? Fuck you think this is?"

She loved the pain mixed with pleasure and within five minutes he exploded inside of her as she came on his pulsating dick at the same time.

When he was done, she flopped on the sofa, bare assed, and looked up at him. Out of breath she said, "That was wrong on so many levels."

"You have no idea what wrong is," he responded thinking of all his dirty deeds. "But I like your style."

She continued to breathe heavily. "It was…nice."

He chuckled once as he wiped his dick with his shirt. "Nice huh? That's all I get?"

She smiled.

"You wanna go another round?" He continued. "That is, unless you wanna go home."

She lied face up on the couch. "Go home for what?"

CHAPTER SIX

The forecast called for more snow and most cars were iced in place, unable to move about the city. Minnesota used the moment to get some peace, until Tobias walked downstairs where she was in the recreation room within the Wales Mansion.

When he saw her sitting on the sofa reading a book, he sat next to her. It was close enough for her to know he was still interested, but further enough away to respect her space. "I was looking all over for you. Joey left a little earlier. Packed a bag."

"Yeah, after Wales Island he needed a break. Hasn't been right since we been home."

"Where is he going?"

She shook her head and her gaze remained on the book. "Why? So you can report back to the boss?"

"You know it's not like that."

"How is it then?" She placed the book on her knees. "Are you here to report to him or not?"

"I'm here because...I mean, ever since, like..."

She shook her head and raised her book again. He was boring her intensely. "Can't even tell the truth."

He removed the book from her hand. "Is that why you're avoiding me? Because you think I'm reporting to Bolero? Because I'm not."

"To be honest, I haven't given you much thought since we left the island. It's been months."

He chuckled. "You can't even lie straight." He paused. "Ever since you bathed me and —."

"You rejected me?"

"It's not about rejecting you. I mean...your age and..."

"I get it." She took the book back. "You don't want to be with someone my age. So, leave me alone."

"It's not that I don't find you attractive. You know I do but —."

"What are Mr. Bolero's intentions with my father?" She asked skipping the subject to something more comfortable.

"What you mean?"

"You're obviously here to watch us." She shrugged. "So, what does he want from my father? And our family?"

"I think he's made himself clear."

"After this, will he leave us alone?"

"I don't want to talk about —."

She got up and walked toward the stairwell. "When you're ready to be real with me, maybe I'll be real with you." She ascended the stairs.

Banks sat in his lounge when Mason walked inside, carrying Cuban cigars in a neat wooden box. He was unenthused and still salty if he were being honest about the meeting. "You climbed out the snow, huh?"

"I wanted to see my mans."

He shook his head. "What you want?"

Mason paused where he stood. "Hold up, I know you not still mad about the Trey and Ram thing. We've dealt with worst shit than that."

"I asked a question." Banks poured himself a sweet glass of whiskey and sat in his leather recliner. "What do you want?"

Mason took a deep breath and walked inside, sitting the Cuban box on the table. "I'm having a party for us. And before you say no let me tell you straight up, I won't take no for an answer."

"I don't feel like going to a party."

Mason sat next to Banks, their legs touched lightly. "Can you at least try this for me? Please? At the end of the day we stuck in this shit. Might as well have fun."

"There you go with that dumb shit." Banks moved a little away. "What exactly am I trying again?"

"I want you to pretend it's not all about the money. I want you to remember a time before things got bad when—."

"That shows how little you know about me." Banks took a big sip. "It was always about the money."

"And I get all that. But there was a period when the paper was rolling in and we weren't worried. Security was tight and we had Jersey and Bet on our arms. After that the babies started coming back to back and..." Deep breath. "...we can get back to that period, Banks. It was short but still sweet." He paused. "Can you do this for me?"

He dragged his palm down his face. "What exactly do you want me to do?"

"Like I said, I'm planning a party. I want everybody dressed because it's a special occasion. You with it?"

"Mason, we got shit to do. I don't—."

"Are you with it or not, man?"

Banks extended his glass and Mason poured him another. "If I do this, you gotta stop making crazy ass moves."

"Just trust me. Everything I do is about us. We good."

Jersey walked into her hotel suite after a long day with her adult children, Patterson, Howard and Derrick. Although she chose not to stay in the home with Mason, after catching him fucking Bet on Wales Island, he was under the impression they were eventually going to work their marriage out.

But Jersey had other plans.

When she strutted to the bedroom, on the mattress was a large shiny red box and a gold bow on top. She smiled, lifted the lid and was stunned at the beautiful designer red Fenty dress inside. On top of the garment was a handwritten note:

Wear this for me. – B.W.

Blushing at the amazing gesture, she sat on the bed, with a grin on her face and made a call. The moment she heard his voice her face flushed. "Wow, you really went all out didn't you?" She touched the expensive threads.

"Only the best." Banks said. "For the best."

She sighed deeply. "What am I going to do with you?"

"Whatever you want."

She shook her head. "Loving you is so easy. Why is that?"

"What we say about analyzing every moment?"

The smile disappeared. If there could be one thing said about Banks Wales, it was this…he avoided all heavy emotional stages.

"What I say, or what *you* say?" She asked.

"I've done a lot of things the wrong way. With this, I wanna take my time."

She fell back on the bed face up. "Okay, what about this, we go away for a week. Anywhere. Mexico. Puerto Rico. To be honest I just want to get away with you."

"I wish I could but it's busy on my end. With work and all."

"That's what you call it. Work?" She giggled.

He chuckled.

"I know it may seem that I'm pressuring you, Banks. It's just that, I'm at the point in my life where I need guarantees. I don't want to spend more time hoping the person I care about wants me back. Hoping that—."

"Jersey, I gotta hit you back."

His statement was abrupt and put her immediately on edge. She popped up on the bed and looked out into the room. Was it something she said? *Again.* "Is everything okay?"

"Yeah, but I just have to go. I'm sorry."

"Okay…call me back when—."

Banks hung up before she could finish her sentence. And she wondered if dealing with him was worse than being married to Mason Louisville because unlike her husband, Banks had her whole heart.

"Pops, don't be mad at me," Spacey said while standing in Banks' office. "Talk to her. For five minutes at least. I think she deserves that much. I mean, she is our mother."

Banks was livid.

Of course, he understood his son's position. And at the same time, he made himself clear, he was not interested in reconciling with Bethany Wales. Not now, not ever.

To be honest he wasn't feeling her in the initial part of their relationship either, but he went with the flow. Everything moved so quickly.

One minute he was buying a house from her and the next minute she had taken it upon herself to decorate the interior of his new home. She was pushy and aggressive, but he respected it in the beginning. Because at least he knew where she was coming from.

But now he was done and there wasn't anything else to be said. Being pushy, or aggressive no longer was cute.

Dragging a hand down his face he said, "She got twenty minutes, Spacey. But I want to make clear to you, that I'm through with your mother. Shit ain't ever going back to what it used to be."

He nodded. "Thanks, Pops."

When Spacey turned to leave Banks grabbed his arm. "This is a favor to you."

Spacey nodded again and quickly exited before his father changed his mind.

Five seconds later, Bet entered. Her hair was all over her head and she looked like an emotional wreck. But her ex-husband, on the other hand looked good. His light skin was without a blemish. The fresh white t-shirt, grey sweatpants and LV slides he donned gave him an easy going look, and she hated him for his apparent ease.

But looks could be deceiving, because the moment he saw her eyes, he knew he was in for a ride.

On the exhale, he stood up straight and crossed his arms over his chest. "What's up?"

She smiled. "What you up to today?"

"What you want, Bet?"

She shuffled a little. "I'm sorry about your car."

"Bought another one."

She swallowed. "I...I also wanted to say that I understand why you're ending things with me. I understand why, why we can't be together no more."

"*Ended* things."

"Huh?"

"You said *ending*. And I need it clear that we over."

She looked down. It was obvious her plan was to come over and speak to him civilly, but that strategy had gone out the window. "I get all that. But, I mean, I just want you to know that I found somebody else." She studied his face like it was a blackboard with a calculus lesson she was trying to understand. She was hoping that she'd see one ounce of emotion.

But Banks didn't utter a word or make a facial move.

The woman was lost.

"Did you hear me, Banks?"

"I'm waiting on the part that involves me."

She stepped closer. "I, I just want to know if, I mean, before I move on, with this new man, I...I need to know if there's anything I can do to bring you back to me. To work on our marriage. The last thing I want is to get involved if you want me back."

He took a deep breath and decided it was time for a bit of compassion. After all, she did bare his last name and she was the mother of his children. And for that he would always take care of her financially and physically if someone disrespected.

Despite her frantic energy, he felt she deserved a bit more. He wanted her happy. Just not with him.

"Listen...I want you to move on with your life." He held her shoulders and looked down into her eyes. "I want you to get with this new man and show him your best. You deserve peace, Bet."

His touch gave her hope and she wanted to kiss his fingertips. "But, Banks…we can work this out. Please?"

He shook his head and removed his hands. "No...we..."

SPIT FLEW IN HIS EYE FROM HER LIPS.

"What the…"

"Fuck you!" She yelled. Her calm demeanor gone. "I know you have somebody else. And when I find out who she is, I will ruin her life and scratch her from this earth."

"Spacey!" Banks yelled, realizing that he was moments away from killing her. "Come in here!" He snatched tissue out the gold holder on his desk and wiped his face. Every fiber in his being wanted to slap her, and if she didn't leave in the next minute, he would do just that.

"Yes, pops!" He rushed into his office.

"Get her out of here!"

Luckily Spacey moved quickly because Bet was preparing to hit him again. It was clear that her rage was so high, she couldn't contain herself. She wanted him back so badly, she would've plucked his eyes out if her nails were longer just to prevent him from seeing another woman.

"I'm sorry, Pops."

"Get her the fuck out my crib before I box her up in a casket!"

"Yes, Pops."

"Now!"

Hearing the commotion, Tobias ran into the office wielding a gun. "Is everything okay, sir?"

Banks grabbed another tissue and wiped his face. "Come in." He looked at his weapon. "And put that up." He tossed the used tissue in the trash.

Tobias tucked his gun under his shirt. "Yes, sir."

Banks leaned against the front of his desk and motioned for him to take a seat.

He did.

"Bolero, tell me more about him."

Tobias sat back and exhaled long. "To be honest I don't know him personally. I mean, since I've known him, he was always around. So, we were used to having him as a staple in our lives."

"And his client?"

"I'm going to be honest again. I was told he was my father, but I have personally never met him. And neither did my sisters. All he ever gave us was a saying, *Con el tiempo serás un recuerdo.*"

"What does it mean?"

"*In time you will be a memory.* But who he was talking to when he originally made the statement, we never really knew." He sighed deeply. "That's the extent of my knowledge."

Banks believed him. "So why did you agree to come clear across the country to represent a man you don't know?"

"Minnesota. I'm here for her."

Banks nodded and sat in the chair behind his desk. "That'll be all. You can go." Tobias rose and walked toward the door. "And, Tobias."

He turned around.

"I'll be keeping an eye on you."

"Sir, I wouldn't expect anything less."

CHAPTER SEVEN

Things may have been icy on the ground, but all Nidia saw were blue skies and white clouds as she sat inside her personal jet, looking out the window. The view was spectacular. In the air was the closest she felt to peace and so she flew often.

And still, this trip was all business.

"You must be smart," she said softly still looking out the window. She was wearing a tight black sweater dress, and her eyes were hidden in midnight shades. "This man…this person, is unlike any you've dealt with before." She turned her head and faced her two female passengers. "Your worst mistake would be to think you're smarter than him."

They were known as the Feathers. And their extraordinary beauty, although shocking to some, shielded their unique talents for murder.

Jennifer and Sophia Featherstone were twins who were raised by a loving mother and a sweeter grandfather. But it was their grandmother who washed the innocence out of their soul to prepare them for 'the real world'. As their grandmother's daughter, their mother, prayed to the Lord above, she taught her

WAR 5: KARMA

daughters to hit their enemies when they weren't looking. And always when their victims were at their most vulnerable. And when their grandfather, her husband, showed them the importance of the bible, she showed them how to whisk up tasteless poisons instead.

Many wondered why a grandmother would teach her grandchildren such violent things. To them she would simply say, *"Because I can."*

Jennifer wiped her naturally long brown hair over her shoulders and crossed her legs. "We will bring you Mr. Wales' head. I don't have to know how smart he is to make you this promise."

"Bringing me his head is the least of your concerns." She eyed her closely. From her viewpoint she could see unearned arrogance in her eyes. Sure, she may have killed a few men in and around her hometown. But this was the major leagues. "Do not let your ego get you trapped. It would be a grave mistake."

"I'm sure my sister doesn't mean to be arrogant," Sophia added, raking a hand through her braids. "But we always get who and what we want." She shrugged. "It's the reason you hired us."

"True. But make no mistake. I will get my money's worth whether you kill Banks Wales or not."

Jennifer glared. "What's that supposed to mean?"

"I don't mince words and I won't start now."

Sophia adjusted in her seat. She heard tale about Nidia's ruthlessness and had no intentions on her sister or herself being on the receiving end of her wrath. At the same time, she didn't see any harm in speaking her mind.

"My only question is do you want him dead?" Jennifer asked. "Because, well, at some point you say bring you his head and then—."

"Yes…I want him erased."

"We will do a good job," Sophia said. "You can trust us."

Nidia nodded and looked out the window. "You won't be able to get at Banks right away. You have to take your time. You have to be calculating. If he gets one whiff of a trap, he will kill you both." She laughed. "And if that happens, well, I guess this will be a one-way trip to your graves."

Howard and Bet walked past the velvet rope and into the plush club known as The Viking. She didn't know where he was taking her but since she was rejected by her husband, she welcomed the distraction.

And a distraction was exactly what her spirit ordered.

The moment she was led inside, her breath felt trapped in her throat when she bore witness to the red and black leather walls. The mirrors were outlined in gold and many silk beds were speckled throughout the joint. It was a synergy of a gigantic bedroom and an elite nightclub.

She was so in awe that such a place existed, that her jaw hung open until Howard grabbed her hand and led her deeper inside, where she could get an even closer look. And it was here that Bet fell weak in the knees.

A regular, Howard adjusted his brown butter colored leather coat and white gold diamond chain as he escorted her further inside. The man was perfect. The Lou men were handsome, messy things.

"Is this a...swingers spot?" She smiled.

"Got a problem if it is?"

He led her to a bed where they could post up and watch the scenery. In many areas of the club people openly had sex. In others, they watched, while sipping on something strong.

There was a couple doing doggy style toward the back. To the right, another man had a woman's legs spread wide as he ate her pussy, as if he were eating a watermelon. In the center two black men had one skinny white woman, one with a dick in her mouth, the other in the ass, as she handled them with the precision of a Mercedes engine.

"You come here all the time?" Bet asked, unable to take her eyes away.

"What happened?" Howard asked as he got situated in place.

"Huh?" She heard him, but her eyes had so much to enjoy. So much to see.

"You were sad all day yesterday, after you saw Banks, so what happened?"

Now her heart ached again. Why did he have to bring up the past when the present was so tantalizing? "He doesn't want me anymore."

"I thought you knew that already." He looked her over.

"It doesn't make it hurt any less."

As he spoke, a stranger walked over, sat on the bed and removed her shoes without an introduction or invitation. With that he softly massaged her feet, as if she ordered him. His boldness and touch sent chills throughout areas of her body she didn't know existed anymore.

"You have to stop pushing so hard." Howard said as if nothing were happening. It was obvious that this was the norm at The Viking. "No man wants a woman so aggressive."

"It's easy for you to say." She smiled at the man, while talking to him.

"Why?"

"Nobody in your family is rejecting you."

He thought about raping her son, which she didn't know about, and Mason's isolation ever since. "I know what it feels like to be rejected. And it don't bother me. I don't go around begging people to talk to me either. I let them come to me when they're ready."

"Then you haven't been rejected by somebody you care about enough."

"You have no idea what I've experienced," he glared at her.

She closed her eyes as the stranger continued to go to work on her other foot. His touch felt electric. "But I—."

"Go away!" He told the man when he saw her attention leaving.

The stranger looked at Bet. "You want me gone?" His question was directed at her, ignoring him.

"I won't ask you again," Howard said through clenched teeth. The man left slowly, and Howard moved closer, which was a sign for others to know they weren't accepting visitors for the moment. "You shouldn't have gone to the house. You wearing your feelings on your sleeve."

"You do know I'm older than you right? I've experienced more. Maybe you don't know as much as you think about life."

"Age went out the window the day you sucked my dick."

She glared and moved to get off the bed. "You know what, fuck this shit. I'll catch a cab and—."

He yanked her arm. "Sit down."

"Get off of me!"

His face turned evil. His voice authoritative. "Sit...the...fuck...DOWN!"

She complied but backed up a little. "What you want, Howard?" Something about his forcefulness reminded her of Banks.

"You need to get back into his good graces. But not the way you've been doing it."

"Didn't you hear me when I said he won't talk to me?"

"He won't talk to you because he doesn't trust you. So, the job becomes making him trust you again."

"And how do I do that when every time I see him my heart breaks? And he throws me out or leaves the scene."

"I don't know." He shrugged. He was honestly tiring of the pity party she was determined to throw. "But that's what you have to find out."

She could feel her face heating up with the fear of rejection. Suddenly, she didn't care about being in the club anymore. "I'm so lost. I spent...spent so much time with him that I don't know who I am without him."

"I'll help you." Howard waved two men over who had been eying them all night. "You won't be alone." He grabbed her hair and released his dick from his pants. He was already rock hard.

"Howard, here?" She asked looking around. "In front of all of these people?"

He pushed down on her head until his dick disappeared between the tunnels of her lips, while the first man pulled her pants down and eased into her pussy. The unexpected feeling, and the pain she felt in her heart, sent her on waves of ecstasy.

The second man stood in front of him and Howard sucked his dick softly. Bet was stunned and turned on as she looked up. It was easy to understand the source of her confusion. They had been having sex back to back, and his body always responded to hers.

If he bisexual, who cared?

She felt so good Banks was an afterthought.

If only for a moment.

CHAPTER EIGHT
THE NEXT NIGHT

It was party time...

The theme...ALL BLACK LIKE THE OMEN. Because Mason had deemed the night, *Death To The Past*. Chandeliers hung from the ceilings and gold poles were set up in every corner of the room, with women swinging from them like branches on an oak tree in the wind. These females were pros; their bodies melted into the pillars as they danced.

The room was already on fire but when the guests of honors stepped through the doors it erupted into cheers. They were on top of the world. Evident by the applause, waves and the guests chanting their last names.

"Wales, Wales, Wales!"

"Lou, Lou, Lou!"

First, Mason, Derrick and Patterson stepped onto the stage dressed in black jeans and black t-shirts. Their necks were draped in different variations of gold and diamonds so that when the light hit them, and it did, they sparkled. One thing was clear. They were steeped in dope money and they wanted the world to know.

Behind them were the Wales clan and it was another story all together.

Banks stepped inside with a black on black Hemsworth suit. The scent of expensive cologne fused into his skin caused women to smile when he walked by. People looked at every inch of his frame, and there was no hint of him being a woman.

Behind him was Spacey, wearing black slacks and a button down, one gold watch for his wrist. On the right of him was Joey who chose black designer jeans so smooth they looked like silk and a black Versace shirt.

The girl of the group couldn't be out done wearing a dress with a slit that raised higher on her thigh than Banks preferred but it meshed with Minnesota Wales' new persona perfectly. Her hair was in a messy bun that would free itself with luscious curls if the right man pulled the pin that kept it all together.

Be careful though, touching her was an honor and a curse.

To her left was Tobias, dressed in a black tuxedo as if he were looking for his bride. Shay followed up on the rear waring a short mini and a smaller button up halter which was dying to open, which would expose her breasts.

"Wow," Banks said looking around at the party, and the excited crowd. "You went all out!" He yelled to be heard over the thump of the speakers.

Mason placed one hand on Banks' shoulder. "We dope niggas. Let them worship us."

As they walked through the party, they were greeted with *handshakes* and *thank you's* for the newfound wealth. After all, the money from Bolero's coke had been so good, some were able to send their children to elite schools, buy eight-bedroom homes and a luxury car for every day of the week.

After greeting their guests, they bounced across the room where a VIP section was roped off in red velvet and gold. Above their heads were lights hanging from a sheer black ceiling, making it appear as if they were sitting below the stars.

Where they belonged.

Once they were all seated, female bartenders dressed in next to nothing, approached the guests of the night. Drink orders were gathered as dancers stood outside the ropes, eager to get any of their attention.

Tobias, the Latin papi, wasn't interested. He only had eyes for Minnesota and preferred to be closer to her than the .22 that she had nestled on her concealed thigh, that no one knew about.

As the party kicked up a notch, Banks eased over to Mason and asked loudly, "Where's Jersey?"

At that exact time Mason waved over a cutie on the outside who sat on his lap. "She been tripping lately. Haven't even been home. I think I'm done with that bitch."

Banks smiled. "You sure?"

"Couldn't be surer."

THE OTHER END OF VIP

Tobias leaned over closer to Minnesota. "You look beautiful."

She looked at him and smirked. He actually looked edible also, but she had yet to forgive him for rejecting her on the island. And so, she dismissed him with her eyes and leaned in the opposite direction.

He sighed. "When are you going to talk to me?" His accent caused her heart to melt. He was so sexy, the women outside VIP wanted at him.

"Talk to you?" She smiled and shook her head. "I don't even know if I can trust you."

"You can."

She rolled her eyes. "I'll know when the time is right. Right now, all I hear are words." She rose and walked away making sure to make her body talk in the process.

"Damn that woman." He said under his breath.

STILL IN VIP

As Derrick sipped on a glass of whiskey, Shay did her best to rub her leg against his thigh. Ever since they returned from the island, she never gave up hope that they would be together. But his mind was on other things.

Irritated, he sat his glass down. "Why you keep staring at me like you the DEA?"

The lights hanging above caused her eyes to twinkle. Let's keep it real, she was a cutie. "So, you really wanna fake dumb, Derrick?"

"I told you we not fucking with each other no more. How many times I gotta keep telling you the same shit over and over?"

"I get all that, but I don't understand why."

"Because you one of *them* and I'm a Lou."

She frowned. "Are you kidding me? They made up. Not even beefing no more. So why shouldn't we be together?"

He waved a waitress down who quickly filled his glass, having committed his drink of choice to memory. "You don't get it do you? This shit they doing won't last." He looked over at Mason and Banks who were heavy in conversation. They were laughing like kids. "Because they will always find a reason to hate each other again."

She moved closer. "Derrick, what we shared back on the island was —."

"Over."

"Was over or *is* over?"

He shook his head, got up and walked away from VIP.

Patterson was close behind.

ON THE DANCE FLOOR

A smooth slow song blasted from the speakers as Derrick danced with a dark chocolate beauty with a banging body, wide eyes and a cute little nose. He noticed her the moment she walked into the party, but it was the innocence, she seemed to possess that had him desiring to get to know her better. A niece to one of Banks' most trusted soldiers, he had to be easy going if he was gonna lure her to his bed.

And so, as they moved, he gripped both of her ass cheeks like a game controller as he looked into her eyes. "I didn't know they made new houses over there. I thought the area was built out." He said, continuing a conversation they were nursing.

"The white people tried to keep development under wraps," she looked at him and then downward. "But we got the last home."

"We?"

She giggled and it made her cuter. "I live with my son. Alone."

"Wow, how old is he?"

"Five."

He nodded and held her tighter. He could deal with a five-year-old. It was babies that gave him the jitters.

"It won't be a problem will it?" She asked. "Me having a kid."

"Why would a single mother who just moved her son into a new house be a problem for me?" He shrugged.

To be honest for some reason he was still thinking about Shay at the moment. And felt annoyed because of it. She was the mosquito bump he couldn't get out of his mind.

"I don't know, it's just that some men don't—."

"I'm not some men."

She smiled. Outside of being fine he was perfect in that moment. "I know. Not trying to lump you in with the others."

"You could never lump me in. My name is Derrick Louisville." He suddenly became extremely cocky. Split personality like.

She frowned. She couldn't stand arrogance. "What is wrong with you?"

"What you talking about, shawty?"

"When you first approached, you acted like you were interested but now it's like you got a chip on your shoulders."

"Because bitches be tripping."

She released him. "Excuse me?"

"You heard me."

"I don't—."

Before she could finish her sentence, Shay had rushed up behind her and snatched four wefts of hair out the back of her head. "GET OUT OF HERE!" Shay yelled; fists clenched into knots. She dropped the bundles on the floor.

The chocolate beauty was about to attack until she realized the woman who did her dirty was a Wales. Instead of retaliating she took to running out of the room, leaving Shay and Derrick alone on the dance floor.

"Fuck is wrong with you?" Derrick asked pointing at the door. "Huh? Her uncle works for Banks!"

"You think I'ma sit by and watch you soak up another bitch in my face? I shoulda killed her." She placed a hand over her heart. "What is wrong with you?"

"In your face? I left you in VIP!" He pointed to the area as if she didn't know where she came from. "Go back!"

"You didn't leave me anywhere. I'm a Wales and —."

"You're not a fucking Wales! Your mother and father dead and Uncle Banks felt sorry for your orphan ass. Other than that, you ain't nothing but another bitch getting on my nerves. So, stay the fuck up out my face!"

ON THE OTHER SIDE OF THE DANCE FLOOR

Minnesota was alone at first, until a mid-level drug dealer decided to make a step her way when he couldn't stand to see her without getting closer. After having a little alcohol courage, Myrio walked up to her rubbing his hands together before saying, "You're beautiful."

"You stared me down for five minutes and that's what you come up with?" She asked.

"You not feeling it? Should I try harder?"

"It's weak at best." She laughed. "I mean, my being beautiful gave you enough motivation to step to me?"

"What that mean?"

"If you don't know royalty when you see it, you don't deserve to be in the room."

"Whoa." He chuckled once loving her rich ass style. "You put me in my place."

"Ain't about that."

"I want—."

"Listen, right now, you have about ten niggas ready to snipe you." She interrupted. "So, if I were you, I'd start the rest of my life making better decisions. Do yourself a favor and bounce."

When Myrio turned around, he saw the Lou's looking in his direction. She was royalty indeed and as a result was treasured.

He was shaken but not stirred. "I know just talking to you means I can die."

"Correction, I can have you killed."

"I get that too." He continued. "But you miss 100 percent of the chances you don't take."

"You like playing with your life? Your odds are better jumping out a plane with no parachute."

He smiled and nodded harder. "I'ma die anyway. Are you worth it?"

The fact that he wasn't scared, made her feel him even more. She had a place in her life for the courageous type. Always. "Do yourself a favor and walk away."

"I won't."

"But you should though."

He stepped closer. "I won't."

Her pussy jumped a little.

"Can I help you with something?" Tobias asked, walking up to the duo. His Latin steeze screamed *Goodfellas*.

Myrio smiled without even looking his way. "We gonna see each other again, Ms. Wales. And when we do, you will be mine." He walked away.

"Who was that dude?" Tobias continued.

"Does it matter?"

"You a boss and you keeping time with the help? Don't seem too smart to me."

Minnesota laughed. "Just because you wearing a tux don't mean I'm your wife." She crossed her arms. "What are you? Jealous or something?"

"It ain't about being jealous. It's about—."

"What you want, Tobias? Huh? I offered myself to you and you shot me down. I'm moving on with my life."

"Not without me you won't."

"You know what…" Minnesota exited the party and walked briskly down the hallway, with him on her trail. When she got to the elevator and hit the button, he was still there.

Looking and smelling good.

"I'm gonna see you to your room." He said.

"Tobias, you don't have to see me anywhere. I'm done with you."

"When you turn eighteen, I will show you all the things I can't right now."

"Don't…don't…please stop." He hurt her feelings and she despised him for it.

He stepped closer. "I have sisters, Minnie."

"Minnesota."

"I have sisters, Minnesota," he was so close she felt the warmth of his body. "And I want them to be respected like I'm respecting you. But don't push your future husband away. You will regret it in the future."

"I'm not your sister."

"That much is true."

When the elevator dinged, and she stepped inside, taking a deep breath. "Age or not, you had your chance. With Minnesota Wales, you don't get another." She hit the button and the doors closed in his face.

WAR 5: KARMA

CHAPTER NINE
DEATH TO THE PAST PARTY

The celebration was in full mode when Jersey came through the scene. She was a showstopper. A jaw dropper and the room had Mr. Wales to thank for sending her in the proper way. Because Banks had observed every curve of her body in the past, he chose the perfect red dress to captivate every line, corner and inch of her frame.

Low neckline.

Low backline.

And a slit to the side that exposed her entire thigh.

Slowly she dipped toward VIP knowing that every man and woman in the room was in awe. When she made it to the section, it was Banks who rose to let her in, even walking her to her seat. Besides, who else? Her sons were on the dance floor along with the other Wales' so for now it was just Jersey, Banks and Mason.

Instead of giving her the props she was due, Mason said, "The color was black."

She laughed. "You look good too, Mason."

Mason shook his head and walked out of the section as Banks moved closer to Jersey. Not too close though.

They had to be careful. All eyes were on her, which meant all eyes were on him by association. Together the two resembled movie stars in old Hollywood and he felt proud to love her in secret.

"Fantastic." Banks said, without looking at her face. His gaze on the dancefloor. His heart on her.

She blushed, loving the way he said each syllable. Glancing over at him slightly, her breath fell heavy in her throat. Banks looked edible. "Amazing."

He smiled and ran a hand down his face. "Mason thinks you look good too by the way. Just putting on for me like he don't care."

She frowned. Just that quickly he ruined the mood. "I don't wanna talk about him when I'm with you. Ever."

"I know his response hurt, Jersey. Despite what's going on between us, with me you can always be real."

She faced him. "I didn't wear this dress for him. Like I said, I don't care what he thinks."

He grinned. "What you sipping tonight?"

"Nothing."

He frowned. "That's the fourth time you refused a drink. Something up?"

Mason returned sloppily with liquor in hand. "Just had to get all the attention on you, huh?" He asked Jersey. "Black was the code. Not red. "

"Mason, stop."

"Stop what?"

"You made everything tonight beautiful." She complimented him. "I mean look at this place. Can't we just enjoy the moment?"

He glared. It had him sick to his stomach that she had stolen the show. Especially since she wasn't checking for a nigga.

"Mason, relax, man," Banks said trying all he could to keep his composure.

"It ain't about relaxing."

"Then what's it about?" He shrugged. "If you got me out here, just for it to be another day in the hood I coulda stayed home."

Mason swallowed all of his drink and gripped Jersey in a rough one arm hug. "Everybody calm down." He planted a wet liquor induced kiss on her cheek, taking some of her blush with the act. "Jersey knows I'm—"

She pushed away from him. "Stop." She wiped away his kiss with the back of her hand. "I hate when you drunk."

Mason yanked her back and Banks saw black.

He was preparing to fuck him up until out of Mason's view, Jersey squeezed Banks' hand softly, to calm him down. It took some time, but his heart rate crept back to normal, the longer she held on.

When Banks reclaimed his position and dignity, she directed her attention toward Mason.

"All I want is to enjoy the night, okay?" She said softly. "Please don't do this, baby."

He glared. "You cheating on me?"

Her heart thumped.

Banks moved uneasily.

The answer was yes and they both knew it.

"What you talking about now, Mason?" She said. "I'm here with you. I thought we...I thought we were working it out."

"You smell like another man."

She glared because she knew she showered. "You cheat on me with Bet and I'm the guilty one. You — ."

"Fuck it," Mason said before exiting V.I.P.

Luckily for her, she said the magic words and there was no way he was going to have her utter them in front of his best friend, making Banks angry all over again.

When they were alone, he took a deep breath. "I started to fuck his ass up."

"Don't, please."

"I'm sorry 'bout that shit. I hate when he acts like that."

She looked straight ahead, to be sure no one saw them speaking. "It's not your fault."

"It's all my fault. I complicated things by — ."

"*We* complicated things, Banks. *We did.*" She looked at him. "You're the best thing that ever happened to me. And if you say the word, I will leave with you. Forever. You know that right?"

He did. "Leave with me now."

Time stopped upon hearing those words.

And without hesitation, she rose, and they exited the party. Together.

Mason may have been pushed up on another female across the room, and didn't see the exit, but there was someone watching it all.

His name was Derrick Louisville.

And he didn't like what he was seeing one bit.

CHAPTER TEN

B et sat in her apartment looking at reruns of the *Real Housewives of Atlanta*. Every time they flashed their shiny cars and massive rented homes, she grew incensed. She felt the women were faking while this was her life.

Well, it used to be anyway.

After pouring the rest of the wine into her glass, she called an old friend. One she abandoned well before she got with Banks. Erica tried to reach her several times throughout her marriage but Bet brushed off each of her calls. After all, at the time Banks Wales and her growing family was a full-time job. She didn't have time for single women or friends.

That was many years ago.

And she regretted her decision.

After letting the phone ring a few seconds, to her surprise, she answered. "Erica? Is that you?"

"Bet?"

Bet laughed. "Yeah, girl! How you been? It's so good to hear your voice! I been...I been thinking about you and was like, let me see how she's doing!"

"Oh my, God! How long has it been?"

When the show flashed a luxury truck, like the one she crashed trying to run down Banks on the snowy streets, she turned the set off and sat back. "I been good but better. I can't lie."

"Well I can't believe you called. We were literally just talking about you the other day."

She knew *we* meant their shared friends but since she didn't talk to anyone anymore, she wasn't privy to what was being spoken behind her back. "Maybe we can get some drinks or something at the bar. I mean, if you all have the time."

"Sure, we're here for you girl."

Bet frowned. "What…what you mean, *here for me?*"

"I mean, with your situation and all."

Bet sat up and scooted to the edge of the sofa. "I'm confused on what you saying."

"We all know, Bet." She giggled once. "No need to feel bad though. I mean, I didn't know you were into women but to each her own."

Her eyes widened. "I'm not *into women!*"

"But Banks is a—."

"Trans!"

Erica giggled louder and longer not feeling the difference. She was so amused, it took her a few moments to return to the call. "Whatever you say, girl. I mean, I know this day and age is different but unless that nigga got a *real dick*, then it's a—."

It was time to drag her ass.

"Marco beat you every day for the first year you were with him." Bet started. "Then he shot you in the neck, almost killing you. But I know what you thinking, you finally had him locked up and moved on with your life. But what about your next nigga? Huh?"

"Bet, I gotta—."

"Vonte fucked your daughter and when you caught them together, he made you suck his dick clean when you threatened to call the police. After he just fucked her. Tell me something, how your daughter taste after you kissed his lips?"

"I will beat your—."

"And what did you do? Take him back and put your daughter out. But when they moved in together, you cried for six weeks before you found your next nigga Leon, who fucked every one of our friends." Now it was Bet who laughed. "And when you went to Princess about it, she slapped you in the face."

"You ain't got to come at me like—."

"Banks may have been born a woman. It's true, and it's a situation I thought I'd never have to deal with. But trust me, he's all man. Ain't a feminine bone in his body and he never disrespected me until I..."

Silence.

"Until I..."

"Until what, bitch?" After getting dragged Erica was praying for some new info to tell their friends. But she would be short because Bet hung up.

There was no use in talking to Erica about her relationship nor did she feel the need to explain. She had issues in their marriage but there was no question that Banks was a good person despite their differences. And it was as simple as that.

Grabbing her wine, she exited her apartment and knocked on Howard's door. After five minutes of yelling and banging, he finally answered.

"What you doing here?" He asked, rubbing his muscular bare chest. He was wearing sweatpants and boxers, and she liked it that way.

"I need you."

"I got company."

She smiled and took a sip of wine before pushing her way inside. "Well that works for me too. We can duo a menege' trois while—."

He stopped her at the foyer. "We wanna be alone."

From where she stood, she could see a young man on the couch rolling a blunt. Looking up at Howard she said, "Let me be clear. If I don't have a dick in my ass or mouth at the bottom of this hour, I'll ruin your gay fucking life." She took a larger sip of wine. "Now what you wanna do?"

He took a deep breath and stepped out her way, allowing her inside.

CHAPTER ELEVEN

The party was winding down but those in attendance didn't know it, especially Derrick and Patterson who were so toasted they could barely stand up straight. It didn't stop Patterson from talking shit up in VIP. "So, she sucked my dick and — ."

"Nigga, let me stop you right there," Derrick responded, a palm to the center of his brother's chest. "You not about to waste none of my time lying tonight." He scanned the party. "Besides, I'm still trying to find my body pillow for the evening." He looked at a few of the women who were stragglers and didn't see anything he liked.

"That's your problem. Your sex life some trash and you think it's the same for everybody else." Patterson said.

"Ain't about that. Just don't understand why you feel the need to..."

Suddenly Derrick's voice trailed off when he saw two women waltz into the room. They were perfect but in a way that didn't make them over sexualized like the chicks bumping into each other on the dance floor. Their allure rested in the middle of sexy and classy and he would gladly have either if given a chance.

"Across the room," Derrick said nodding his head toward them.

When Patterson looked toward the entrance, he was stunned himself. To the brothers the women were strangers. To Nidia they were known as the Feathers, and they came with ulterior motives in mind.

"Go get 'em," Derrick said, wiping his hands down his pants.

"Why I gotta go?"

"If I get up, I'm taking both of 'em."

Patterson knew his brother was serious, so he jumped up to complete the chore. As he moved, he could smell the many shots wafting from his pores and hoped the women wouldn't be too turned off. And then he remembered who he was, Patterson Louisville.

It was an honor to smell his drunk ass, to hear him tell it.

When the Feathers saw him approaching, Jennifer whipped her hair over her shoulder and Sophia allowed her braids to hang down her back.

Feeling like Sophia resembled more of a bad girl, he directed his attentions to her. "You ladies look like you're lost. Can I help you with something?"

Sophia smiled, and then ran her tongue over her lips. "Was driving by and saw beautiful black people coming and leaving." She eyed him seductively. "Figured it looked like the place to be."

"We wrapping up but if you wanna grab a drink with me we can go from there."

Sophia looked at her sister.

"I ain't got nothing else to do." Jennifer replied.

Patterson walked the two women over to VIP where Derrick was waiting alone. Since it was obvious that Patterson and Sophia had made a connection, Derrick directed his attention toward Jennifer instead. He made quick introductions and the rest was all she wrote.

"So, where you from?" Derrick asked, after he made sure the bartenders gave them a glass of something strong.

"New York," Jennifer crossed her legs. "But we're looking for something a little slower paced. So, we may get an apartment out here."

Minding his brother's business, Patterson whipped his head toward her. "You saying we slow in Maryland?"

"I'm saying it's too fast in New York," she corrected him, not accepting the word play trap. "There's a difference."

"Aye, man, focus on your date," Derrick said.

Patterson rolled his eyes and chatted it up with Sophia again.

"So, what you getting into tonight?" Derrick asked Jennifer.

"Are you asking if I'll let you take me home?"

He chuckled. "You get down to the point, don't you?"

Jennifer stood up. "Not really. I just don't see any reason to play games. Do you?"

Derrick rose.

Following their queue, Patterson and Sophia stood up too and walked toward the exit.

With Shay glaring from afar.

CHAPTER TWELVE

The window was open inside the luxurious suite, allowing the luminescent moonlight to shine through. It was the perfect ambiance for secret lovers.

Jersey sat on top of Banks' thickness, moving up and down slowly. Her gaze remained on his and the passion they felt couldn't be placed into words. There had never been a woman before and he doubted there would be one after, who could make him feel whole.

He was so in awe, for a moment he thought about his first girlfriend. It's true, Nikki loved him, but she denied him early on. To the day he wondered what might have happened to their relationship, had her first boyfriend not died. And then there was Bet, who from the get-go saw a cash cow and went at him full force.

But Jersey knew all about him. She knew his struggles. Knew his crimes and more than it all, knew his heart. And still she stayed.

Still she wanted him.

"Banks, I..." She pumped slowly up and down. "I never want this to end." She nibbled on her bottom lip.

As he felt her warmth, his hands found her hips, as he enjoyed how she snaked so that the flat part of the dildo stayed directly in place on his body, necessary for him to reach an orgasm.

"I know." He moaned.

"Do you?" She moved a little quicker and then slower. "Do you really?"

"I feel you. This shit is right."

And with that their bond was professed without saying the words. It was real and dangerous, but they couldn't stay away from one another.

When they were done making love, she laid next to him and rubbed his yellow tatted, muscular chest. "I want to say something about…you know, you being a —."

He smiled. "I'm not like I used to be. Say what you feeling."

"What you mean you not like you used to be?"

"Sensitive."

She was surprised. "I never knew you to be sensitive. You always seem in control."

"I cared about too much. Wasted a lot of time. I don't care so much anymore."

"Why?"

He exhaled and wiped her hair from her face so he could see her eyes. "You're beautiful." He softly skipped the subject. "Do I tell you enough?"

She blushed. "All the time. But you make me feel it even more when I'm in your arms."

He kissed her lips and took a deep breath. "When I first found out that I was...different, I didn't have anything to base it off. I knew of one other trans person in my building as a kid but we never talked. And so, I looked at my situation like, like a curse."

"Banks, I—."

"No, let me...let me finish." He breathed deeply. "I wanna talk about it now. No more hiding. No more...running from my story."

She smiled.

"I realize now that for whatever reason, we stuck with who we are." Banks continued. "But who we become is up to us. This is me and I don't give a fuck who knows anymore. I gotta live my life and that goes for everyone."

She touched his face and ran her hand down to the dildo. It was warm, soft, thick and now wet. It moved under her fingertips with ease. "This thing feels real."

He chuckled. "Got five more like it in the closet."

By T. STYLES   111

She laughed heavily. "I bet you do." She considered things a little more. "Can you get a real one? If you wanted. With your money."

"The surgery chances are better now. And I thought about it." He shrugged. "But it could fall off if the blood flow doesn't stay right and I could die."

She frowned. "Fall off? Yuck!"

He chuckled. "You see what I'm saying?"

She nodded. "I like what we do now, especially since you can—."

"Cum?" He said.

She nodded yes. "Can you?"

"Harder than you know," he responded.

"When I look at you, I don't see anything…anything like a woman."

"What you see is who I am."

She sat on top of him again, hands planted into his chest. "And who are you?" She listened to his heartbeat and voice.

"A man, really feeling a woman for the first time in his life."

The air left her body in one big rush. "Wow…I…never thought you would really confess how you felt. I thought you felt bad about—."

"Mason?"

"Do you? Feel bad."

He nodded. "I die every time I think about what we're doing to him. And then I'm revived when I see your face. I love that nigga, like a brother, but he opened the door to this shit right here. Not me."

"So, I'm revenge?"

"Can you really ask me that?"

She looked down. "I'm concerned about us." She said. "I don't want to lead Mason on when there's nothing there for me anymore."

"I get you."

"So, what does that mean?"

He exhaled deeply. "Mason is a dangerous man."

"I don't care about him being dangerous. He's—."

"But you should though." He paused. "I'm serious. He's a *very* dangerous man who, who will destroy you if he ever finds out about us."

"You think he would hurt me and not you?"

"Yes." He said. "He will always choose me over everybody else."

"So, we keep this a secret?"

"For now, we play it smart. But trust me, Jersey, I'm thinking. I'm thinking hard. The idea of having to share you with anybody fucks with me in a way I'm not accustomed."

She giggled.

"What?" He frowned.

"It's just…it's just crazy that Bet and Mason cheating brought us here."

"I think we've always known something was between us. Let's just ride it out."

She nodded. "Agreed."

CHAPTER THIRTEEN

Slightly bigger than Banks' home, Mason's new mansion was spectacular.

Two weeks ago, he closed on an all brick mansion in Baltimore County that stunned everybody who came near which was exactly the reaction he was aiming for. Every area of the home was designed to perfection and Mason spared no expense.

But it was his kitchen that dropped jaws.

Mason had it organized so that twenty people could sit across from the chef and see the food being made comfortably, as they enjoyed a meal. And that's what was happening now.

To celebrate making big money, the day after the party, Mason planned a massive breakfast. He had every food imaginable on the table. Pancakes, crepes, French toast, mimosa. The man was on top of the world.

When Derrick, Patterson and the Feathers came downstairs dressed in pajamas, preparing to eat, Mason grinned with pride. He caught a look at the beautiful young ladies at the party last night and definitely approved. But now, in daylight, they were still stunning.

"Damn, Pops," Derrick said rubbing his belly as he eyed the meal. "You went all out." He yawned.

Mason nodded. "It's the after party. You know how we do."

"I'm still hungover." Patterson said rubbing his head. "Glad you hooked us up because I was gonna go to Micky D's."

"You ladies hungry?" Mason asked.

"Sure," Jennifer said tucking her hair behind her ear.

"I can eat too," Sophia responded. "Can I make a fruit punch? So, I can help."

"Knock yourself out." Mason winked.

Sophia quickly walked to the cabinet to grab a pitcher and the ingredients as Mason and the other's held a conversation.

Jennifer, knowing what she was doing to the punch, made sure to keep everyone engaged.

When the tasteless poison was added, Sophia placed it in the refrigerator claiming it tasted better cool, before taking her seat.

Besides, the drink was made especially for Banks Wales, who she knew was coming later based on her conversation with Patterson. But whoever else decided to sip the treat could die too.

She simply didn't give a fuck.

After eating lightly, the quartet sat at the table and before long Jersey entered through the kitchen door. "Where you been?" Mason asked.

A deep breath. "I'm here now." She washed her hands and sat at the table. "Why, did I miss something?"

"I don't know, did you?" Derrick asked with a lowered gaze.

She glared. "You have a problem, son?" She grabbed a plate and a piece of bacon, confused at her son's reaction.

He shrugged. "I don't know. I mean, are you still a part of this family? Because I don't understand why you don't choose to stay home anymore. Seems a little off to me for a woman with kids."

"Ya'll grown."

Mason chuckled. "Stop being serious, Jersey. He just playing."

Jersey rolled her eyes and looked at her husband. "So, you think it's okay for my son to talk to me that way?"

Mason sighed. "Like I said the boy was just playing."

"The boy is a man who's being disrespectful." She looked at the ladies. "And we have company at that.

That's a terrible impression to be making don't you think?"

The Feathers looked away, eyes on their meals. They were there for murder not drama.

"Sir, Banks is here," the maid said walking into the kitchen with him following behind her.

"My nigga," Mason said excitedly, strolling up to Banks. Everyone in the room was aware that Mason was nowhere near as excited until he saw his best friend's face. "Fuck took you so long?"

"I don't know, Pops, seems like perfect timing to me," Derrick interrupted looking at his mother and then Banks although the question was not directed at him.

Banks frowned. "You okay, nephew?"

"Why wouldn't I be, Unc?" Derrick said.

Banks ignored him, trying to keep his good mood intact.

"What you drinking?" Mason asked. "Got Mimosas."

Banks walked to the fridge. After the morning fuck session, he and Jersey had, he was thirsty. He was so focused on quenching the feeling that he didn't see the two guests. "Need something a little lighter right now." He pulled it open and smiled when he saw the juice.

Grabbing it out of the fridge, he walked it to the counter to pour himself a glass.

Sophia and Jennifer were so excited their legs trembled under the table. The plan was to pour him some personally, but this was better. If consumed, the poison would not take effect until three hours later, and they would be long gone.

The anticipation made them wet.

Could it be this easy?

"So, what ya'll been up to?" Banks was about to take a sip when he saw the two women. Sitting the glass down he said, "Who they?"

"Friends of the boys," Mason said proudly. "They fine ain't they?"

Banks wasn't sure, but there was something about them he wasn't feeling. "Oh yeah?" He stared at them intensely.

"Yep, they made the juice and everything." Mason said.

Now Banks looked at the pitcher and the glass in his hand. On impulse, he poured the cup and the jug in the sink. It gulped loudly going down the drain.

"Why you do that, Unc?" Patterson asked with an attitude. "My friend hooked us up."

"Do I really gotta remind you about Wales island?" He said, referring to how Arlyndo died. "No new niggas around me."

Suddenly the mood was dark. And sad.

Of course, everyone remembered.

Banks sat far away from Jersey as possible, but it didn't stop their eyes from meeting. "I'll drink mimosa."

Jennifer and Sophia realized Nidia was right. Getting at him would be easier said than done. But with having the fellas wrapped up, they felt they had all the time in the world.

After eating their meal, Mason slapped his belly several times as if it were a drum. "Wow, that was great!"

"I can't lie, it definitely hit the spot," Banks said rubbing his chest before burping once.

"Good job, Mason," Jersey smiled, wiping the corners of her mouth with an expensive linen napkin.

"As much as I would love to take credit for everything I can't," Mason paused. "Gotta thank the chefs for that." He pushed back in the chair. "But what I can take credit for is outside in the driveway."

Derrick frowned. "What's up, Pops?"

"Come with me and find out."

When they followed Mason, they were standing in front of his five-car garage. There were five Mercedes Benz trucks in silver, gold, blue, red and white. He looked at his sons and rubbed his hands together as if trying to start a fire. "Pick what fits and I'll throw the rest away."

By throw the rest away he meant he'd have his dealer pick them up. A move reserved for big bosses and the rich.

His sons were so excited they almost tripped over themselves trying to get at the new rides. Patterson ran to the gold while Derrick dipped to the red.

Jersey sighed. She felt that once again Mason went over the top, and at the same time she couldn't help but smile when she saw the looks on her sons' faces.

Jersey and Banks approached Mason.

"You couldn't wait to tap the bag, huh?" Banks said shaking his head.

"What we agree too?" Mason asked him seriously.

"Come on, man."

"I'm serious. I thought we would get this money and if it wasn't working tap out. Until then that means to have fun and that's what I'm gonna do."

Banks nodded. Being reckless with money was not easy for the man but he made a promise to at least try.

Besides, a hint of guilt forced him to humor Mason a little more.

"Let a nigga live." Mason continued. "It ain't like Bolero ain't hooking us up."

"You not lying." Banks agreed. "I'm just surprised we were able to move most of the weight so fast."

"It's quality coke," Mason nodded. "You can cut it ten times and it would still feel pure."

Across the way, Patterson and Derrick had eased behind the seat to each car in the driveway before Derrick settled on the blue and Patterson the white.

"So, you giving one to Howard, too right?" Jersey asked Mason.

"What I tell you about asking me about that nigga?"

She frowned. "When are you gonna tell me what happened between you two? It seems like since we got back you —."

"If you bring him up to me again, I won't be liable for what I do next."

"Easy, Mason." Banks warned. "She just asking."

"And I'm tired of talking about it. So, leave it the fuck alone." He stormed away. Jersey's confused gaze remained on him until he disappeared into the house.

"You okay?" He placed his hand on the small of her back.

She smiled the moment she felt his touch. "I am now."

And once again, Derrick saw it all.

CHAPTER FOURTEEN

Banks walked inside his house, only to see Mr. Bolero sitting on the sofa, smoking a cigar. His maid stood in front of him, trembling with fear. "You let him in my house?"

"I'm sorry." She said softly. "He said it was urgent."

"We'll talk later."

"Mr. Wales—."

"Later," he said interrupting her. When she walked away, he said, "What you doing here?"

Mr. Bolero took a deep breath. "I got these here, in America." He raised it and put the fire out in his hand, before putting the cigar in his coat pocket. Didn't even flinch in pain. "They can never make them as good as Cuba though."

"What are you doing in my house?" He walked in front of him and stood taller.

"I'm here about your friend."

Banks frowned. "What friend?"

"Mason."

Banks crossed his arms over his chest because short of fucking his wife, he considered Mason a brother. "What about him?"

"He's causing too many problems."

Banks ran his hand down his face. "The deal was to move coke. We doing that. So, problems should be a mute issue if the money flowing."

"I agree. You're doing a good job."

"Exactly. So why you bothering us now? We didn't agree to be your boys. We agreed to move work."

"That still doesn't mean a little micro-management isn't necessary."

Banks sat in the recliner to gather his thoughts. He was quite aware that the man he was dealing with could cause problems for him and his family. Which is why he agreed to the proposal in the first place. And so, he wanted to avoid issues. At the same time, he was nobody's employee.

"What part of Mason you got a problem with?"

"He's flashy."

"He a dope dealer." He shrugged. "Almost comes with the territory."

"And that's my issue. He even went as far as to use my name on the streets. At the end of the day, his actions effect mine and my client's."

Banks frowned and sat back. "No, he didn't use your name. He'd have no reason to mention you."

"If I said he used my name he did." Bolero removed his phone from his pocket and tapped a few keys. Within seconds, a known voice was on the line. It was white boy Trey. In the past he was a friend of Banks', but after Mason embarrassed him in front of Ramirez in the motor home, things took a turn for the worst.

In the land of the hoods, White Boy Trey even took to making soft threats on the streets toward Mason. And Banks promptly gave word, that if a hair on Mason's head was truffled with, there would be war. All of this was done without Mason knowing.

Most who were smart decided to stay out of the beef altogether.

"Trey, I'm here with Banks." Bolero said. "Tell him what you told me,"

"How you know Trey?" Banks asked Bolero, ignoring the call all at once.

Bolero sat the phone face down on the couch. "That's of no concern to you." He raised the phone. "Trey, what did you tell me?"

From the phone Trey said, *"Banks, what's up?"*

Banks glared as if Trey could see his face.

"I'll take it that you fine since you won't answer." Trey cleared his throat. *"I told Mr. Bolero that Mason was*

making it out that both of ya'll are cocaine kings and that Mr. B was the plug. People I know been looking for him ever since. To cut you two out the deal and snatch Bolero."

Banks was irritated beyond measure. Could Mason be so stupid?

"To answer your earlier question on how I know Trey it's simple. He found me." He said to Banks, before ending the call without a goodbye. "And if he can find me, the DEA can too. Get a hold on Mason. Or I will." He stood up and walked out.

Unable to get on the Wales Estate property, Sophia and Jennifer sat outside in a rental on the street. When they saw Bolero drive away in the backseat of a Maybach, they sighed.

"We should try to get inside now." Sophia said softly. "Shoot him straight up and get this over with. We can be home by the new year."

"Nidia said he's smart," Jennifer responded, continuing to look at the gates surrounding the property. "So, we have to be smarter."

Sophia sighed. "Why do I get the feeling you like being here? With Derrick."

She laughed. "You have to ask yourself that question. I'm about this work."

"Listen, Derrick and Patterson *are the work*." Sophia said seriously. "Don't get too comfortable. It may get you killed."

"So, what you suggest?"

"Pry a little harder with Derrick. Maybe we can find out where Banks will be and kill him then."

"Banks is always with someone, even if they aren't in the room, he got somebody watching him outside the room. You saw that when we went to breakfast. He had two men in the distance, looking our way." She pointed at the house. "Look at the men now. They are walking the property like he the president."

"That's why you need to get into Derrick's head. Patterson doesn't know much. It's Derrick. Work him and work him hard, Jennifer."

CHAPTER FIFTEEN

Derrick, Patterson and Howard were hitting their mark at the gun range. It was a past time they all shared before Arlyndo died, and they wanted to keep the tradition alive in his honor.

"She was wet before I even touched her," Patterson bragged as they exited the range and walked toward Derrick's blue Mercedes truck. "That bitch wanted it bad. Been dicking her down ever since the party."

As Patterson and Derrick spoke, Howard couldn't get over the new truck that Mason bought him sitting in the driveway. He knew they were given new rides from Mason, and it fucked him up hard. In his opinion Mason was deliberately trying to hurt his feelings and at times he thought he was going too far.

"Fuck Pops get ya'll new trucks for? Ya'll already had this year's models."

"Please don't act like they ain't sweet." Patterson said as they all climbed inside, with Derrick behind the steering wheel. "You know you want one too."

Derrick pulled into traffic. "Howard, what the fuck is going on with you and Pops for real?"

Howard readjusted in the backseat. "What you mean?"

Derrick frowned. "Nigga, you moved out. And far as I can tell, Pops been playing you distant."

Howard shrugged. "I'm grown. Fuck I care what he thinks?"

"We grown too. But niggas not leaving before it's time." Patterson added.

"But you should though." He paused. "I don't want Pops and Ma running my life forever. I mean think about it, the way he got things, the moment you don't do what he wants, he'll cut you off payroll."

Derrick scratched his head. Howard was on to something. At the same time, they would rather drain the cash until it was no more than to leave the nest.

"But you ain't answer the question. What ya'll beefing about?" Derrick continued.

There was no way on God's green planet that Howard would express what he'd done to Spacey. When they first came home from the island, he wondered how much Mason told anyone. It soon became obvious that he hadn't said a word to a soul, not even his mother. And he would keep it that way.

"He mad I wanted my own spot. I don't know why ya'll keep asking me the same shit though. It's annoying at best."

Derrick pulled into the bar parking lot. "Yeah, ma would freak out if we moved out too." Patterson said. "But she gonna have to deal with it sooner or later. Because if shit works out with Sophia, I may be ready to make that change."

"Nigga, shut your broke ass up. You gonna be in the house just like me." Derrick parked. "I gotta tell ya'll something, about ma."

Both frowned.

"What's up?" Patterson asked.

"I think...I think something may be going on with her and Banks."

Patterson busted out in laughter, while Howard maintained a tight face.

"How you figure?" Howard asked.

"Nigga, it don't matter how he figures," Patterson said. "Ma ain't fucking with no Banks Wales. She still on Pops' dick, trust me."

"If you say so," Derrick said.

"Hold up, ain't that Bet?" Patterson asked as he looked at a banged-out car following them into the lot.

"Yeah, fuck she want?" Derrick glared.

"I'll find out." Howard unlocked the truck door. "I'll meet ya'll inside."

"You sure?" Patterson asked.

He nodded. "I got it."

As everyone piled out the truck, Patterson and Derrick took one more look at Bet before walking inside.

Howard rushed up to her, grabbing her by the elbow, yanking her a few feet away from the bar. "Fuck wrong with you?"

Since he was close, he could see the gaze in her eyes. She looked zoned out. Slowly she raised her hand and smiled, before touching his cheek lightly. "I wanted to…talk to you."

When she touched his face, he felt something wet. At that time, he saw blood on her hand. Grabbing her arm, he saw her slit wrist.

She fainted.

Bet was lying in the bed, her wrist bandaged. When she opened her eyes, she saw Howard standing at the open window, looking out at the purple night sky.

"You stayed?" She said in a soft voice. Her throat was dry, and she was extremely thirsty, despite the I.V. in her arm.

"I want to tell you something. Something you should know. About me and Spacey."

She looked away and closed her eyes. "I know already."

He frowned and leaned against the wall next to the window. "What you mean *you know*?"

"I don't have the details but, I mean, I saw you two together one night. I walked into his room and he was lying on his stomach with you on top of him. He seemed zoned out and I figured it was something you two did all the time. So, I let you both be."

He walked over to the chair and flopped down. "And you don't have a problem with it? You didn't care that—."

"I'm never gonna judge my son because he's different. Plus, to be honest, after we had sex, I thought you grew out of the gay stage. Until the club."

"I'm not gay!"

"Whatever." She looked at him and shrugged. "And Spacey seemed to develop a craving for big pretty women. So, I wouldn't say I don't care. I just thought it was a phase you both were going through."

He was shocked and at the same time there were so many things he wanted to know. Starting with her suicide attempt. "Why you do it?"

"I told you I didn't want to interrupt you two when—."

"No, not me and Spacey. Why you hurt yourself?"

She sighed deeply. "Because I'm trying to protect the world."

"From what?"

"From whatever I'm about to do next."

"Well, before you do anything, I have to tell you something you need to know. It's about my moms and Banks."

CHAPTER SIXTEEN

Banks sat with Mason in the basement of Mason's home. All around them were cash machines stacked with money. It was a boring, tiresome job to count paper. And their fingers were gritty to the touch, but they didn't trust such an important chore to anyone else. Besides, if any percent was off, they wouldn't be paid and as a result would have to forward their cuts to the boss.

"Bolero stopped by my house the other day." Banks placed a rubber band around a stack and grabbed another mound.

"Fuck his old ass want?" He dropped a bunch of cash and hit the button for the counter to start.

"To talk about you."

The money machine rung in the background as Mason sat back in his chair. "Why am I the topic?"

"He said you been mentioning his name on the streets. To niggas who don't need to know."

Mason shrugged and removed the counted stack, before bounding it with a band. "Bolero not even from this country. What difference does it make who I talk to? He should be —."

"I'm with you, Mason. You know I am. But sometimes you don't think straight. This ain't about just making money and paying the debt. This is about being set up for life."

"I get it."

"Do you?" Banks sat back and crossed his arms over his chest. "You always said you admired my island. And how I was prepared to go when shit got thick. I got it by thinking about the future. And not busting my money on trucks for—."

"What I do for my sons—."

"Has a place." Banks interrupted. "What you do for your sons has a place, Mason." He leaned in closer. "In the meantime, leave Bolero's name out the talk. That's an order. It makes him uneasy and until I find out why—."

"You mean *if* you find out why."

"*Until I find out why*, be easy." Banks continued. "I'm working on info about that nigga."

"Who said something to Bolero anyway?"

"It doesn't matter."

Mason nodded and counted a few more stacks. His thoughts went ahead of him, on every man past and present who Banks wronged. He also thought of those he'd wronged too. The list was extensive but with a little narrowing down he was on the one.

Suddenly he smiled. "You know they found White Boy Trey dead in an alley off Reisterstown Road last night, right?" He looked at Banks with knowing eyes. "You know anything about that?"

Banks shrugged. "Nah."

Mason smiled, having gotten all the answers he needed.

Mason, Banks and Jersey sat in the back of Club Life in the outskirts of Baltimore City. It was an invite only type of organization that tailored to the rich and privileged. How you came about your money was of no concern to the club. It could come by drugs, real estate or pussy. The only thing that was important was that you had class when you walked through the doors.

And Banks fit the bill.

Mason, not so much, but next to his friend he still shined.

As they popped bottles, Jersey's favorite slow song boomed from the speakers. She looked beyond sexy for the evening, wearing a tight black dress that dipped and smoothed over every curve.

Mason sat back proudly in the lounge chair as he looked at her pump her body on beat. She had recently gotten bohemian locs and looked like a cute young thing without a care in the world. Just the way Mason liked her.

She could have any man, but she wanted Banks Wales.

Although she was near, she wasn't close enough to hear what was being said between the friends.

"Damn, ain't she fine?" Mason said.

Banks looked at Jersey dancing and nodded in agreement. He felt the word 'fine' was a bit weak but for now it would do. "You acting like you just met her."

Mason frowned. "I'm talking about the bitch across the room, not Jersey's ass." He shook his head. "You don't see the red bone with the donkey ass?"

Banks shifted a little. The girl was easy on the eyes, no doubt, but in his opinion, she had nothing on Jersey Louisville.

"You keep Jersey busy." Mason said as he wiped the corners of his mouth. "I'm gonna see if I can slip her my number."

Unaware of the conversation, Jersey continued to move her body for the only person who mattered in the building. Except now, with Mason gone, she was staring directly at Banks. The sexual tension between them had reached fever pitches and both felt like they were children in a candy store.

As Mason walked away to pitch for another bitch, Jersey didn't even look his way. Instead, she swung her hair ever so lightly over her shoulder, touched the top of her head before snaking her hands down her body while resting at her hips. Jersey was a dime. He'd always known but now it was plain to see.

"You're so fucking sexy," Banks whispered, hard enough for her to read his lips over the music.

She mouthed. "So are you."

He winked and sat back and watched her rock out the entire song.

Suddenly, when he blinked, she was covered in blood. Her hair. Her face. Shoulders. Arms and legs. The vision sent chills down his spine. So much so that he jolted up and blinked several times to bring himself back to the present.

"You okay?" Jersey asked, seeing him breathe heavily.

When he looked at her now the vision was gone. And she was gore free.

Her kind eyes rested on him with confusion and concern. "Banks, what's wrong? Are you okay?"

"Yeah, I'm...I'm good." He dragged two hands down his face.

"You look like you saw a ghost."

Banks' eyes rested on Mason who was still talking to the woman across the room. Did the blood on Jersey's body represent something deeper? Involving Mason, Jersey and a murder.

Sort of a premonition of things to come.

"I saw worse than a ghost."

"I, I don't understand."

"We gotta be careful. I'ma leave it at that."

Smooth rap music played in the background while Derrick, Patterson, Jennifer and Sophia sat in booth style seating in the lounge. Sophia was propped up on Patterson's lap while Jennifer and Derrick sat closely to them on the other side.

"...nah, it's not like that," Patterson continued, talking to the group. "I think you can have a girlfriend and a wife if everybody agrees. What's the problem?"

"You do realize I'm not the girlfriend type, right?" Sophia said. "And I'm definitely not the wife type."

"Luckily for you that's not a bad thing seeing as though I'm single and plan to stay that way." Patterson squeezed her ass.

"Can you tell your brother he's digging himself into deeper holes?" Jennifer whispered to Derrick. "My sister may be interested in giving him the time of day if he wasn't so gross."

"You can't tell that nigga shit." Derrick shrugged. "I don't even think he had pussy before meeting Sophy that night."

Patterson laughed having heard his sibling. "Go on 'head with that shit, yo. You and me both know what the deal is."

As they continued to have light conversation, Sophia looked at Patterson with penetrating eyes. "Tell me what you do for a living?"

Patterson sat back. "We playing?"

She shrugged. "Nah, I really wanna know."

"We deal in pharma—."

"Shut up, nigga," Derrick said, cutting Patterson off before he dropped all the deets.

"But she already knows." He replied. "Look how we living."

"And I said shut the fuck up." Derrick said firmer. "It's alright to kick it a little. But leave it at that."

Jennifer looked at Sophia as both of them deflated. There entire purpose of meeting the Lou's was to get more information on Banks. But it appeared that Derrick was smarter than they gave him credit. And because of it he would be a problem.

"Hold up, ain't that Shay?" Patterson said pointing at the door in front of the lounge. "She looking good too."

Derrick squinted and turned a different shade of black when he saw her angry face. He rose quickly. "Let me rap to her stupid ass."

Within seconds he was grabbing her by her elbow and escorting her toward the back of the spot. "Fuck is you doing here?"

She yanked away and crossed her arms over her chest tightly, as if she were wearing a strait jacket. "You think you gonna post up with this bitch and —."

"And what?" He stepped closer and hung over her head like mistletoe. "Live my fucking life?"

She tilted her head upward. "I'm not letting you be with no whole new bitch, Derrick. I done told you that. Consider this a warning."

"You ain't got to *let me do shit*. It ain't your place."

She looked across the room. "I don't trust her."

"It don't make no difference. You can't stop me from doing me. Besides, I been told you we don't fuck with each other no more. It's…"

He continued to talk but Shay's focus was elsewhere. Still across the room, where Jennifer was smiling sinisterly her way.

"…because what we —."

Shay interrupted Derrick's sentence by giving him an open kiss in the mouth. It seemed like forever and he didn't fight back.

When she was done, she separated from him and said, "What we shared on Wales Island was real, and I'm gonna stay around until you figure shit out. And you *will* figure it out. Because you need me. And I need you. But don't make me wait too long. I'm growing impatient." She walked out the door.

Mr. Bolero stood in a rented office with his soldiers. On the desk in front of him were eight bags filled with cash that his accountant sorted through endlessly. On the other side of the table were Banks and Mason, waiting for the total they both knew was accurate, down to the dollar. Besides, they counted the money themselves.

When the accountant was done, he took a deep breath. His fingertips gritty like sand due to the dirty bills. "It's all here."

Bolero smiled. "My client will be pleased that you were so successful with the first batch. You can expect the next batch at the end of the week. We—."

"Yeah, yeah, we know." Mason said interrupting. "Anything else?"

Bolero was incensed at his disrespect.

Sure, their connection was business only, but he wanted the hood nigga to be at least enamored with who he was. A very powerful man. And at the same time being kind was not part of the plan. It was all about the money and both of them came through.

Still, Bolero looked at Banks, hoping he'd calm Mason down a little. But unlike in the past, Banks felt it best to fall back and let a goon be a goon.

"Anything else?" Banks repeated.

Bolero sighed. *"Con el tiempo serás un recuerdo."*

Banks frowned, having learned the phrase from Tobias. He got chills.

"Fuck that mean?" Mason said. "English, my nigga. Speak English."

"Leave it alone," Banks responded, although he knew.

Banks nodded at Bolero as they both walked out.

Mason's mansion was fully loaded with an indoor-outdoor pool. It fit the ambiance perfectly, as suddenly Banks was in the mood to celebrate. Normally he would play it calm. But after divorcing his wife and getting into a strange business relationship with the mysterious Bolero, he was tired of being the levelheaded one.

For once in his life he wanted to live and *ACK A FUCKING FOOL.*

And so, as Mason threw an indoor pool party consisting of Derrick, Banks, Jersey, Patterson, Sophia, Jennifer, Minnesota, Tobias, Shay, Spacey and a few women who flirted around in next to nothing bathing suits, he posted up, arms draped along the back of a recliner, eyeing Jersey who was staring directly at him.

The gaze was explosive and passionate.

"Sir," Jennifer said walking up to him. Her tone was soft, but her intentions were deadly. The plan was simple. Get him to trust her so that she could get closer and then take his life. "Can I talk to you for a minute?"

Banks glared. Angry she interrupted the eye fuck game he was playing with Jersey. "What you want, girl?" He didn't bother to look her way.

His tone attacked her ego. "Did I do something wrong?"

He looked over at her. "I don't know, did you?"

She sat in the recliner next to him. "I understand that you—."

"Get up."

"Excuse me?"

"Get up and walk back over to my nephew. And never talk to me again without an invitation."

She rose slowly, her face warm to the touch due to embarrassment. At the same time, she had a job and she had every intention on carrying it out. With or without his help.

Still, she had to return to the drawing board.

Derrick Louisville.

CHAPTER SEVENTEEN

Banks walked into the house exhausted beyond belief as he spoke to Jersey on the phone. Ever since he let his guard down, he was having more fun with her and time seemed to pass by too quickly. To be honest, Banks' life was so tumultuous as a young man that he never got a chance to fully live until now. Being afraid of what his father would do next as a child, put him in extreme anxiety as an adult and so he was always in preparation mode.

He prepared for the future by stacking cash.

He prepared for a family by marrying a woman who would allow him to live his dreams fully.

He prepared for their futures by sending them to the best grade schools and colleges.

He prepared for their safety by planning their escape to Wales Island.

He prepared for the seriousness of life by avoiding fun.

But now he was done with being *responsible*, for the moment anyway.

Walking into his office, he smiled as he continued to listen to Jersey's soft voice.

"I know you think I'm tired. But if I'm making you a promise, I have all intentions of keeping it."

"What does that mean?"

He chuckled. "It means I'll see you tonight."

"Really, Banks?"

"Wouldn't miss it for anything in the world."

"You sure about that? Because I've been wanting to be alone but lately it's been about me, you and Mason. Like we're in a boy band or something."

He chuckled. "Nah, I just use anything or anybody as an excuse to see you."

"Tonight, Banks." She said firmer. "Don't make me wait."

When the call ended, he sat the phone down on his desk and dragged a hand down his face.

"Pops, you okay?" Minnesota asked as she walked into his office.

He smiled and sighed deeply. "Come in, baby girl. How you doing?"

She smiled, eased inside and sat on his lap. "I'm good. Just, just trying to take it easy." She looked at him closely. "I see you're having fun. I like it on you." She looked down at her fiddling fingers. "Especially since Harris…"

"I know." Losing his son still bothered him a lot, particularly in the quiet moments. "Still think of him every day." He took a deep breath.

"You sure you aren't doing too much?"

"So, my daughter is about to lecture me on being responsible." He joked. "Is that what this is?"

She shook her head softly to left to right. "No, I'm happy you like this. I mean; you always work so hard for us. Always poured everything into this family that, I don't know…"

As her sentence trailed off, he looked deeper into her eyes. "What is it, Minnesota?"

"It's mom."

He tapped her thigh softly for her to get up, and she did so quickly, sitting on the sofa across from him. "What your mother and I have going on is —."

"She's here."

He dragged his hand down his face. This shit had to fucking stop. Not only was he done with her, he was done with her using the kids to get to him. Not to mention the fact that all of their children were mostly grown, so at the end of the day there was no reason for them to speak to one another.

Ever.

"Minnesota, I don't love your mother anymore."

"Dad —."

"Listen," he raised his hand. "I don't love her anymore, but it doesn't mean I don't care about her. Now I'll speak to her for you, but I don't want you thinking it'll be anything more. And I don't want you to put me in this position again."

"But why is it over?"

Of course, he knew the reason but talking to his youngest about it wasn't something he was willing to do. And didn't he do this for Spacey already? What was going to change?

"People grow apart. And that's what happened with us."

She nodded.

He remembered something else was on his mind. "How are you and Tobias?"

She blushed, too embarrassed to say more. "We okay...what...I mean..."

"I know how you feel about him and I know how he feels about you."

"How...I mean —"

"Tobias asked me about you. Wanted my blessing."

She pushed a strand of hair behind her ear. "What did you tell him?"

"To wait until you're older."

"Do you trust him?"

He nodded. "Yeah. I do."

She was shocked. He trusted no one. "Why?"

Deep breath. "I'm not gonna lie, at first he seemed to be coming onto your mother at the island. And he was. I saw it. I realize now that he came from poverty and you do what's necessary to rise. But when things hit the fan on Wales Island, he was there for us. And he made a few moves against Bolero's intrusive behavior recently that I like. So, it changed my opinion. For now."

She stood up, kissed his cheek and walked to the door. "What about mom?"

"Send her in."

She nodded and walked out.

Five seconds later Bet eased inside. Her wrist was bounded in gauze, and she looked like she hadn't eaten in weeks. "Bet, I have no problem with you seeing the kids at the house, with the exception of Minnesota they grown anyway, but we don't have—."

"Let me stop you there."

He leaned back in his seat.

"I'm not here to beg you to come back to me, Banks. Besides, I did that already and it didn't work."

"You said that the last time." He threw his hands up. "And then you put me in a position where I almost laid hands on you."

"I'm here to say everything makes sense now." She said holding her head up high.

"Bet—."

"Just hear me out." A palm was thrown in his direction. "I mean, you owe me that much."

He didn't but okay.

"I used to think there was something wrong with me. But now that I see clearly, I know it's not me. It's you."

"Bet, I don't have time for—."

"You're fucking Jersey. Aren't you?"

He stood up and slightly stumbled.

And just like that, she shook the great Banks Wales.

She smiled. "I want you at my apartment tonight, Banks. I have a list of things I desire, including money, time and sex. And you will pretend you want to be there and give me everything."

"What if I don't?"

"You may be fucking Mason's wife, but I know why you're doing it." She leaned against the doorway. "Because sleeping with her, is the closest you can get to fucking your best friend. Just like he did with me." She shrugged and smiled brighter. "Although, I don't understand why you two just won't get together. And make it easier on everybody else around you. You have a pussy. And he has a dick. Just go for it. We're tired of being used as pawns." She sighed deeper. "It doesn't matter. Be there tonight. Or I'll tell Mason everything he needs to know." She walked out.

When he was alone, he said, "Fuck!" Picking up his phone he called Jersey. "Bae, I'm not—."

"Let me guess, you aren't coming."

"It's just that—"

CLICK.

He looked at the ended call and flopped in his seat. This was the last thing he needed, and yet he couldn't pretend that with Bet knowing about Jersey, that danger wasn't near.

He had to figure out a plan.

Now.

CHAPTER EIGHTEEN

The speakers in Mason's house blasted throughout with music, as Derrick and Patterson entertained the Feathers. The new place was miles away from the old mansion and thanks to the junky Lou's, just as nasty.

Jersey would normally hire a clean-up crew, but her attention was deflected thanks to Banks, who at the moment she was beefing with when he once again cancelled plans.

Before his call, she had everything notched out for the evening. She would meet him at their favorite hotel, where she was at the moment. And they would make love and she would tell him her *special idea*. Instead, she would spend the night crying.

It wasn't like her husband noticed the emotional disconnect. He had gotten comfortable with her isolation. And so, Mason was out with one of his side bitches, the redbone with the donkey ass, which in the past used to drive Jersey crazy. But they were both cheaters now and neither seemed to notice.

As the Lou sons entertained Sophia and Jennifer with drinks by the indoor pool, they didn't have a care in the world. Money was rolling in. Their father seemed happy to be reunited with Banks and they hadn't seen their mother calmer.

And then they would remember Arlyndo. During these moments they would get drunk, smoke weed and pill pop, until the pain went away.

When Sophia slid in front of Patterson inside the pool, she wrapped her arms around his neck and eased on top of his lap as they waded in the water. The moment he felt her heated pussy hanging over him he knew what she wanted. "You playing right?"

She smiled. "You the one playing." She kissed his lips. "You gonna come get this pussy or what?"

The challenge was accepted.

He removed his rock-hard penis from his trunks and pushed into her waiting body. She was warm. She was tight. And she was ready. Up and down she slid, using the water as a glider. The more she pumped, the more he pulsated and before long, he exploded inside her, while sucking hard on her neck.

Derrick ran playfully behind Jennifer in the hallway of the mansion leading to his room. Her angelic giggle was so cute that he did everything he could to make her laugh just to hear it.

When he caught up to her, he pinned her against the wall and looked into her eyes. "You so fucking sexy."

She looked up at him and grew serious. "I like being with you."

He frowned a little. "So why your face say different?"

"I don't know it's just that..." she shrugged. "I feel like you keep too much from me. I mean you say you care about me but it's not what I feel." She placed the side of her face against his beating heart. "I want to know everything there is about you."

"We just met."

"I know, Derrick but—."

"But what?"

She looked up at him. "I dated some niggas before that I cared about. I mean, I thought they were going to be the ones I would spend the rest of my life with."

"*Some niggas?*"

"You want me to lie about my life? And pretend you were the only one. Or can we be real?"

"Never lie to me."

"Good. So, whenever I got with them, there was always a problem. My last boyfriend was arrested on drug charges and I got caught up too. I would've ridden for him had I known but he kept shit from me."

Derrick separated from her and leaned on the wall across from the one she was pinned against. With the hallway between them they felt miles away from each other.

"You wanna talk about my work?" He asked. "That's what this about?"

"Why not?"

"Because I can't put you in on that part of my life. I told you that already. I'm sorry." He threw his hands up. "And if you keep pushing—."

"I'm not pushing."

"You sure?" He lowered his brow.

Silence.

"If you wanna get to know me, then you have to take me as I am." He continued. "Can you deal with it or not?"

Jennifer shut the bathroom door in the pool house and sat on the closed toilet seat. Taking a deep breath, she removed her phone from the cabinet underneath the sink. Dialing a number, it took five calls before Nidia finally answered. "We're still in. Things are running smoothly too."

"You mean you're in with the Lou's?"

"Yes."

Nidia sighed. "That's not what I'm paying you for. I need you closer to Banks."

She readjusted a little. "Banks hasn't been around much."

"Lies." She paused. "If Banks is around any family, it's the Lou's."

"I mean—."

"Besides, from the report Sophia gave me earlier, Banks and Mason are closer than ever." Nidia continued.

"They are but—."

"But what?"

"I don't think Banks is as close to Mason as he is with his wife Jersey." She shrugged. "So, to be honest, he hasn't been here much. Its' even harder to get at him."

Silence.

Jennifer looked at the phone. "Nidia? You there?"

She was but she was incensed with anger. The fact that once again Banks had chosen another woman over her had her feeling a type of way. "Get next to Banks. Fulfill the mission I gave you."

"We won't let you down."

"Kill him within twenty-four hours. Or I'll kill both of you bitches."

Jennifer was on her knees as Derrick pounded into her from behind on the bed in his room. He used her hair as a reign, which he pulled with every stroke. She was wet and her juices were smeared along his shaft as they continued to fuck hard.

"Damn you feel good," he said looking down at her body.

"You, you feel even better." She moaned.

"This my pussy?" A few pumps to the right.

"Yes, it's all yours," she bit her bottom lip as she performed sexually. "It's all…it's all yours."

After a few more strokes, pushes and grinds, they exploded in ecstasy, trying their best to catch their breath. After their session was over, she lie in his arms.

It took less than five minutes for both of them to fall into a deep sleep. Derrick behind Jennifer with his arm hanging alongside her waist. He was a light sleeper, so when the door opened his lids raised.

But no one was there.

Was he hearing things?

When he closed his eyes again, he fell deeper into sleep. And then, five minutes later, he heard a gurgling noise. His eyes flew open only to see Shay standing on the side of the bed, a bloody knife in her hand.

She had sliced Jennifer Feathers soft throat.

Horrified, Derrick popped up and his eyes flew open. "Fuck...what the fuck...why did you do that?" He slid out of bed and backed into the wall. "And how you get in my crib?"

"If my father has keys, I do too." She said calmly, uncaring even.

"This shit crazy!"

"You underestimate how hard it is to be alone." Her voice was soft and off-putting based on what she'd done. "How hard it is to be without you."

Derrick placed his hands on the side of his face. "What you do, yo? Fuck you do?"

"I told you I wasn't playing with you and this bitch. But I'm done with your girlfriend now. I'm done with you too. You can have the rest." She walked out the door.

CHAPTER NINETEEN

Patterson was asleep with Sophia in bed. They had been on a twenty-four-hour sex spree and were beat. You wouldn't know it to see his room now but, in the past, he didn't appreciate the old mansion, until Banks destroyed it with a bomb. Now he was different.

His room was immaculate and cherished. Everything in place.

Patterson just rolled over when suddenly he was yanked out of bed by his brother with a firm hand over his mouth as Sophia remained sleep.

Once outside the room, Patterson shoved Derrick away. "Fuck is wrong with you? I was—."

"Shut up, just, just shut up and come with me." Derrick walked down the hallway briskly, feet slapping against the porcelain floor, with Patterson closely behind. Before long they were in a small room within the basement. And Shay was leaning against the wall, speckled with blood.

On the floor was Jennifer's corpse.

Patterson quickly locked the door. "Fuck is going on?" He looked at the body and then his brother. "What ya'll do?"

Derrick dragged his hand down his face. "It don't matter what we did. The only thing that matters is what we gonna do next."

Patterson felt as if the room was spinning. "Nah, you gotta tell me more than that!" He pointed at the body. "You pull me out of bed and bring me into a room where my girl's sister is spread out on the floor?"

Shay smirked. "So, she your girl now?" She looked at Derrick and back at Patterson. "You Lou's work quick don't you?"

"What, bitch?" Patterson moved to lay hands on her, but Derrick shoved him away.

"That shit you 'bout to do is wasting time." Derrick pointed at him. "We need a plan and we need one now. Before Pops finds out."

The weather was much warmer, and the ice had begun to melt around the outside of the Lou Mansion. Causing everything to sparkle.

Wrapped in a pink cotton robe, Sophia trudged into the kitchen, yawning. She was still exhausted after her and Patterson's love fest and she thought he would be out too. Instead, she found both brothers in the kitchen eating cereal in big bowls with big spoons like children.

Patterson looked over at her, although his gaze was brief. "You were out all morning." He scooped some cheerios into his mouth. More of a way to have something to do than anything else.

After staring at him a bit longer she said, "So, is someone gonna give me a bowl or not?"

Patterson continued to eat until Derrick gave him the death stare. Slowly he rose, grabbed a bowl and spoon and pushed them her way as if she were his kid sister. The cereal came sliding down the table a little later. She stopped the box before it hit the floor.

"Wow, I guess the romance is over." She poured herself a bowl.

The Lou's continued to eat in silence.

"So…" she scooped cereal into her mouth. "Where is my sister?" She wiped milk from the corners of her lips. "Still in bed?"

Patterson choked and coughed a few times. "She…she left. Right…right, Derrick?"

Derrick nodded.

She sat the spoon down and chewed what was left in her mouth. "She would not have left without me."

"Well that's what she did." Patterson shrugged.

Her eyes widened and her heart rate increased. "Something...something ain't right."

"Listen, we had an argument in the middle of the night," Derrick said. "She...she kept asking about my work and—."

"Your work?"

"Yeah, wanted to know what I did for a living and shit like that. And when I didn't tell her she...she got mad and left."

"See," Patterson said. "Now you want me to call you an Uber or what?"

Banks decided against going to see Bet last night. Besides, he needed to get his thoughts together. And although Bet made several threats, he didn't visit her when she requested. Things were still on his terms. Instead, the sun was shining when he entered her apartment. But nothing prepared him for Howard sitting in her living room like he was bae.

Staring Howard down, Banks tucked the key he used to enter her apartment in his pocket. Since he was paying the bills, he felt well within his rights to gain access to the premises whenever he desired.

"What you doing here?" He walked toward Howard and sat in the recliner across from him.

"What you mean?" He shrugged. "Me and Bet are friends."

Banks stared harder. "Shouldn't you get some friends your own age?"

"Shouldn't you?"

Banks chuckled once. The kid was a clown. To be honest he didn't care who she was keeping time with, although he felt the relationship a bit eerie since his father was his best friend. Especially if he was the man she was claiming to be with. "Where is she?"

"Stepped out."

Banks nodded and looked at him a bit longer. Now that they were alone, he had some questions for him. "What happened between you and your father? On Wales island."

He snickered. "Nothing."

"We playing games now?"

He shrugged. "I don't know what you want me to say, Unc." He leaned forward and placed his elbows on his knees. "I mean, I would think he'd tell you."

"Mason doesn't tell me everything."

Howard looked down. "I need you to do me a favor. I mean...if...if you can."

"And what is that?"

"Put in a good word to Pops. For me."

"A request from a man who holds secrets?" Banks wiped his hand down his face. "That's different."

"A son needs his father."

"Then a son should tell him, himself."

"He won't listen."

Banks sighed deeply and rose. He had many things on his mind, and none involved Howard Louisville. "Talk to him again. And leave me out of it." Banks moved toward the door. "Tell Bet I came by."

Howard glared. "You feel bad for how you doing your wife?"

Silence.

"You'll regret it one day." Howard continued. "I'm sure."

"Don't speak on what you don't know."

"One day you'll need me too, Unc. You'll see."

Banks shook his head and walked out the door.

CHAPTER TWENTY

Minnesota and Tobias sat in the dayroom in the Wales Mansion watching TV. Every so often he'd look over at her and she'd catch him. When he did it again, she decided to call him out. "Why you keep looking at me?"

He chuckled once. "You know why."

She grabbed the remote and turned the TV off. "Let's stop playing games, Tobias."

"Oh really, you wanna keep it real? Finally."

"A few months in America and already you saying *wanna*?"

He laughed and her heart flipped. His voice. His accent. All hit the right chords. "You're right. It's just that I'm surprised that you finally want to go there."

"Go 'head."

"Minnie!" Shay said running into the room breaking up their flow. She was sweaty and her hair was unraveled, and it was obvious she was going through some things.

"Minnesota." She snapped, angry she interrupted Tobias. "And this better be good."

She held her palms out. "I'm sorry, Tobias...and...it's just that... I need you both to come with me."

She rose. "What's going on?"

"I'll explain when we get there."

Banks was driving down the street when he received a call from Mason. He quickly answered. "What up?"

"Ain't shit." He yawned. "Just finished taking a nap and decided to go grab a bite to eat."

Banks chuckled once and shook his head as he continued to steer the car. "So, you're calling me because..."

"Guess who having breakfast with me this morning."

He frowned. "Who?"

"Bet."

Banks quickly pulled over to the side of the road, almost striking another car in the process. A few horns beeped in anger and continued down the road. "I thought…I thought you were done going there with my ex."

"Nigga, she popped up on me and I immediately hit you." He paused. "I ain't 'bout to play these games with this chick no more."

"Mason, relax," Bet said in the background.

"That was her right there?" Banks asked.

"If you mean is she sitting at my table and not getting up, the answer is yes."

"Let me rap to her right quick."

A few seconds later Bet answered. "Hello, Mr. Wales."

"What you doing, Bet?" He asked hysterically. "Do you really wanna go there with me? Knowing I can cut you off for life financially?"

"Banks, you killed me inside. What I care about living and having money? It's over." She said calmly. "And you know what I'm talking about. Make it happen."

He ended the call and tossed his phone in the passenger seat. "FUCK!"

Derrick, Patterson, Spacey, Tobias, Minnesota and Shay stood over the body in the basement which now begun to stink of rotting flesh. The Wales clan was shocked that they were seeing the corpse of a woman.

"Where is her sister?" Minnesota asked the Lou's.

"She left." Patterson said.

"What happened?" Tobias questioned.

Patterson glared at Shay who looked away. "Somebody thought shit was sweet enough to kill her. Just because she was jealous and —."

"Leave her alone," Derrick said pointing his brother's way.

Patterson frowned. As far as he knew his brother wasn't interested in Shay but now since Jennifer was gone, he seemed to start feeling her again.

"It doesn't matter what happened." Derrick said looking at everybody. "All I know is this, the last thing my pops needs, or Banks for that matter, is this shit right here." He pointed at the body. "So, I say we get rid of it."

"So why call us?" Tobias shrugged. "Why not bury her yourself?"

"Because a member of the Wales family did this shit." Patterson instructed. "That's why."

Minnesota was focused as she looked at the corpse's greying flesh. "It rained this morning." She said.

"What that mean?" Patterson shrugged.

She looked up at him slowly. "It means the ground is still moist."

The earth was raised, and Jennifer Feathers was placed inside where she would eventually become plant life. The damp dirt covered her body as Shay, Derrick, Patterson, Minnesota, Spacey and Tobias stood around the newly covered hump.

Many things were acknowledged in the silent moment. First, words didn't need to be said. What was done was done and nothing would bring her back even if they wanted. Secondly, they were bounded by this secret, unwilling participants making a decision to bury the past.

Literally.

Minnesota took a deep breath deciding to say a few simple words. "Nothing needs to be said to our parents. Nothing needs to be said amongst ourselves. We are officially letting it go. Forever."

CHAPTER TWENTY-ONE

J ersey planned everything.

Earlier in the afternoon she got bikini waxed at the spa, her hair curled, and her makeup done lightly. After last night she was certain she wouldn't hear from Banks again. And yet there she was, sitting in a luxury hotel room waiting on him to enter after he called.

When there was a knock at the door, she looked down at the tight-fitting purple maxi dress she was wearing to be sure everything was nice. The material clung to her body perfectly which was the plan since she wasn't wearing panties.

Slowly she opened the door and took a deep breath when she saw his face. Banks had always been an iconic figure, but now that he stood in front of her, dressed in all black, smelling like money, he took her breath away as if it were the first time.

He stepped inside, smiled and sat in a recliner next to the window overlooking Baltimore. "Come here." He removed his smoky shades and placed them on the table. "What you drinking?"

"I don't want alcohol." She locked the door and sat on his lap. "How was your day?"

He smiled. Too much had gone on to talk about the details, so he thought it best to make it easier. "Do you remember when we went to that restaurant in D.C. Where them chicks got on the table and —."

"One of them fell trying to dance and shit." She giggled. "Yeah, I remember."

He nodded and smiled at her recollection. "I think I knew then that there was something going on between us."

She frowned. "You knew then? I mean, it was a horrible night. Somebody got shot and everything at that restaurant."

"I know. That was bad, but I was having a fucked-up day before then. Bet had one of her mental outbursts and to be honest I ain't feel like going."

"Mason woulda been mad if you pulled out."

"You telling me? Plus, I knew he was bringing the boys and I was bringing the kids. It was just a long night and then...then I heard your laugh." He wiped her hair from her face and tucked it behind her ear.

She looked down and he raised her chin, so that their eyes met again.

"Just the sound of your voice, just the...just the sound...made everything go away. And I never knew why until we made shit official. Until we made shit right."

"Wow." She took a deep breath. "I never —."

"We can't be together, Jersey. And I'm sorry about that."

She stood up, backed away from him and fell on the edge of the bed. "You said, you said you'd never do this." She pointed at the floor. "I...I don't understand. Why do this to me? Why do this now? Aren't we happy?"

He rose and walked slowly toward her. "I don't want to hurt you, Jersey. But —"

"If you don't want to why...why you breaking my heart?" Tears rolled down her face. "Please, Banks. Don't, don't leave me. You'll take my hope for living with you."

"Something happened the other day, that got me worried."

"For what?"

"For you. Because if Mason finds out. If he gets any idea that we, that we're together, he'll destroy you. And I can't have that." He sat next to her. "I can't have anything happen to you because of me. I can't risk never hearing your laughter again." He placed a hand on her thigh. "It means too much."

"Get out." She said as huge tears fell quicker.

"Jersey —."

"Get out!" She hit him with a closed fist on the leg. "Get out." A hit to the arm. "Get out!" A hit to the shoulder before she dropped to the floor.

"Jersey, I'm sorry. This is the last thing I wanted." He looked at her once more and walked out.

When he was in the hallway, he texted Bet with...

DONE. HOPE U HAPPY BITCH.

Banks dragged himself in the house after being in bars all night. If someone wanted to kill him, it would've been the perfect time, but they missed their chance. He was now home safely, surrounded by his soldiers.

His stomach churned due to a broken heart and he wondered repeatedly if he'd made a mistake by letting Jersey go. But he couldn't lie. Bet had him shook because she was on to facts, although he didn't know how she came about the information.

Jersey was still on his mind when he walked into his house, only to see Mason sitting on the sofa.

"I gotta change my locks." He walked over to the bar and made a drink.

"Even if you did, they wouldn't keep me out. Besides, your maid likes me."

Banks shook his head. "I gotta fire her ass too. What's this about anyway?" He stumbled.

"Maybe you shouldn't drink no more tonight."

"Says the nigga born drunk." He almost fell again when Mason ran toward him, catching him before he hit the ground.

"Go sit down. I'll pour two."

Banks walked to the sofa, flopped down and dragged a hand down his face.

When he was seated, Mason served him up and sat next to Banks. "What's on your mind? You look like you in love."

Banks sat the glass down upon hearing his words. He was now concerned. Did he know about he and Jersey already? "What's this about?"

He took a deep breath. "You remember when that shit happened with my father? The night he died. Where were we going?"

Banks normally steered clear of conversations about the past when it came to Mason. The wounds were still red with blood. But he preferred the past to the present, which included his being in love with the man's wife.

"My pops took us to Burger King." Banks sighed. "I remember like it was yesterday."

"You know, out of all the times we did shit together, that was the happiest day for me."

"Why?" Banks grabbed his drink and took a sip.

"Because I saw the pride on your face. That your father was able to do something for you, instead of me all the time."

Banks nodded and when Jersey's face flashed into his mind, he took a larger sip. "Yeah, that was...it was a day I won't forget."

"But don't get it twisted, the *best day* of my life is when I smashed them drawers." Mason said, reminding him once again about when they made love as teenagers.

Silence.

Banks shook his head and busted out in laughter. "Nigga always talking about the past." He drank all his liquor. "Stay in the present it'll treat you better."

Mason chuckled loudly, having heard Banks' favorite quote. "Anyway, the kids chartered a plane and are sending us to Hawaii. I think we should take 'em up on the offer. Let's get away. Bolero good for now."

Banks exhaled. In his soul he felt like saying no. But what did he have to stay for? The kids were taking care of themselves. He had broken up with Jersey and he was certain Bet was plotting revenge as they spoke.

He figured it was best to stay around Mason, to keep him away from his ex-wife. "Let's do it."

Mason was shocked he answered so quickly. "Don't pack nothing but shorts. We getting everything else there."

The private plane was fueled up and a pilot waited on the runway as Banks and Mason hobbled toward the jet. Both had been drinking non-stop and were loud as they rapped about the best times of their lives as teenagers.

These days Banks Wales was not the same. And he was surprised at how easily it was for him to be carefree and not the most responsible person in the room. But it didn't stop his heart from pumping for Jersey. He missed her. He needed her. And he had to let her go, since he didn't know the time or hour Bet would tell Mason their secret.

Banks and Mason were deep in conversation as they walked toward the aircraft. "So shawty hit me up right and — ."

"She still had your number after all these years?" Mason asked him.

"Hard to believe?"

"Yeah, cause your ass don't cheat."

"My digits stayed the same but..." when they boarded the plane and Banks saw Jersey, he was shocked sober. He turned to Mason. "I thought the kids did this for just me and you."

"I ain't say that." He tapped Banks' back and walked toward Jersey, kissing her on the cheek. "I just said they sending us to Hawaii. Don't trip. We on vacation!"

The plane's door closed before taking flight.

CHAPTER TWENTY-TWO

Patterson's head rocked as he woke up in bed, his face nestled under large pillows. Last night was rough to say the least. He couldn't get over the wide-eyed expression of Jennifer's face being covered in dirt. And then there was Sophia. Ever since he told her that Jennifer had left her in the mansion, she called only once, to see if anything changed. It wasn't until he heard her frantic voice, that he realized he was really vibing with her and at the same time none of it mattered anymore.

After all, her sister was dead.

Sure, after Wales Island he should have been accustomed to death and gore. But knowing someone should die because they wronged you, and seeing a dead body unexpectedly was a different monster altogether.

When he tossed the pillow off of his head, he was shocked when he saw his room was a complete wreck. The TV was smashed, his clothing was kicked around and everything was knocked down or out of place.

"What the fuck?" When he jumped up, he grabbed his head because he was immediately off balance. He had to get himself together quickly because he needed to know what happened.

Running down the hallway, when he made it to Derrick's room, he kicked the door open with the sole of his foot. "Get up!" Derrick roused a little but for the most part remained sleep. This did nothing but anger Patterson even more. "Nigga, get the fuck up!" He yelled shoving him harder.

Derrick held the side of his head and sat on the edge of the bed. "Fuck is your problem? Don't be coming in here, kick—."

"Why you mess up my room?"

"Mess up your room?" Derrick tilted his head. "Fuck I look like, kick—."

"I'm telling you the room is a wreck. TV's smashed. Clothes all over the place! It's crazy!"

"Nigga, I ain't come in your room and do shit. I been in here all night."

"Then who else? Pops and Ma ain't here."

Derrick rubbed his temples again. "Even if they were home they still wouldn't do no dumb shit like that. You sound stupid."

Derrick took a few moments and looked around. Suddenly he had an idea and he wasn't happy about it either. He slipped in some sweatpants and grabbed a jacket.

"Where you going?"

"I'll be back."

WALES MANSION

Shay walked into the dining room where Derrick was seated at the table. She carried two glasses of wine, as if it were a casual visit even though his eyes said he was all business.

When she sat down, she raised her foot and laid it flat on the chair. Taking a quick sip she said, "So..." she shrugged. "Why you here?"

"Derrick sat back and looked up at the cathedral ceilings. "How many meals you think we ate in here?"

She shrugged. "Me and you by ourselves?"

"We never ate by ourselves."

She shrugged again.

"Stop...stop that shrugging shit and answer my fucking questions." He snapped.

She smiled, loving to see him angry. "Too many."

He nodded. "Were you feeling me at any one of those dinners?"

She frowned. "Nah."

"Why?"

"Because, because I was with Harris. Couldn't see past him back then." She looked down. "Never thought I'd have to be without him to be honest."

"You mean you couldn't see past your brother." He corrected her. "Who you were fucking."

"We didn't know at the time." She drank half the glass.

"I heard you still wanted to be with him, even after you found out."

"I did."

"You gross as fuck."

"Why you here, Derrick?" She threw her arms up. "It's obvious you don't fuck with me like that. So why come over now?"

"Why you kill Jennifer?"

She looked behind herself and back at him. "I thought we weren't supposed to be talking about that. If Minnesota heard us she—."

"Why you do it?"

She lowered her brow. "Because you disrespected me."

"We had what we had on the island." He leaned closer. "And I told you when we got back that things would be different. So if anybody was disrespected it was me."

She got up and sat on his lap. "Stop saying the same shit over and over. Derrick, we can have what we had on the island here, at home." She touched the side of his face. "Don't you see? Don't you realize how far I will go to…to be with you?"

His dick hardened. "Is that why you fucking up my house?"

She threw her head back. "Fucking up your house?"

"Patterson's room was tossed up, shit missing, I mean, it's a mess."

"Derrick, I did what I wanted already." She shrugged. "Fuck I look like messing up Patterson's room? What am I two years old? Nah, I decided to let you go after I off'd that chick."

Silence.

"You let me go?"

She noticed his expression seemed disappointed. "Yeah. Why? You feel a type of way now?" She kissed his lips. "Is that why you *really* came?"

"Nah. Just trying to figure out what's going on that's all."

She smiled. "I don't believe you."

He looked into her eyes, and her pussy tingled because it was like he could see through her soul. "I can't lie." He said. "You got my attention."

She giggled. "It's a shame I had to kill somebody."

"The question is, what you gonna do with it now?" He asked.

"Whatever you want." She stroked his crotch.

"I can get pussy anywhere, Shay. I need you to say something different."

"You can't get pussy like mine." She advised. "My shit validated."

He chuckled once. She was cute. "If we do this, whatever it is, never fuck with me."

"And if we do this, never fuck me over." She said. "Because we both know what I'm capable of. Don't we?"

CHAPTER TWENTY-THREE

B et was on hands and knees as Howard pounded into her from behind. The position not only represented a way for him to reach a faster orgasm, but by hitting her from the back, her face was concealed, and he could imagine she was someone else.

Bethany Wales had officially reached the lowest point in her life.

So much had changed since she was divorced. For starters, she had fallen out of the social circles that she was accustomed. Although Banks kept her on a healthy allowance, something he always intended to do whether they were together or not, no one wanted to be around a woman who didn't have access to Banks Wales. So, she was outcast. A social pariah, looking to find her place.

And she found it in the arms of her husband's best friend's son.

"Lower your back more," he said, refusing to see even the waves of her hair fall alongside her face. He wanted only to see her shoulders and ass lifted high.

"I should tell." She said as she pushed back into him the way he liked.

"Tell what?" He fucked her harder.

"Mason."

He stopped pumping because it was evident her mind was not in that room. "Why you say that?" He pulled out and wiped his stiff dick with her shirt.

She laid on her side. "I asked him to come by the other day. So, we could talk about what Derrick told you. And he avoided me."

He sighed. "He did come by. The next morning."

She frowned. "Why...why didn't you tell me?"

"I'm telling you now."

She was angry but it was tough beefing with the only friend she had left in the world. "Even if he did stop by, he took his sweet time."

He laid in front of her and his dick softened slowly.

"It's like, like he thinks I won't do what I say." She looked into his eyes. "It's like he thinks I won't, I won't ruin his life."

He wiped her hair behind her ear. For some reason, when she spoke revenge her eyes lit up in a way that turned him on. "If you do this...if you tell my father about Banks and my mother, there will be war."

She shrugged. "Will there really?"

"Why you say that?"

"What does it mean to have a war, when the two men involved can't stay away from each other? I'm starting to think they are incapable of being real enemies. They are, I guess, in love. Unless I tell Mason this."

He nodded. "True."

"Mason and Banks have fought for years and they always, always, seem to find a way back to each other. But something like this…" She sat on the edge of the bed. "This would set them back forever. Wouldn't it?"

He propped next to her as they both looked at the blank wall as if they could see the battle before their eyes. "How would you do it?"

She shrugged. "As far as I know, Mason doesn't have a direct problem with me. I mean, he wanted to kick me away from the breakfast table the other day but—"

"What?"

"It's a long story." She waved the air. "But this time I'll go over their house and talk to him. Make it like it's about my relationship with Banks and—."

"He's out of town."

She looked at him. "Out of town? With Banks?"

"With my mother too."

Naked from the waist down, she stood up and walked to the wall. "Where did they go?"

"Hawaii."

Her body quivered and she fought with screaming and crying at the same time. "He told me he broke up with her."

"Doesn't sound like he did."

"How does he think, how does he think I will sit by and allow this to happen?" She asked through clenched teeth. "How does he think I will allow him to fall deeper in love?"

"He's not thinking."

Her eyes widened. "This will be the biggest mistake of his life."

He got up and pulled her back to bed. "How much you think Banks will give to keep his secret?" She lied face up and he crawled on top of her.

She frowned. "I don't know but it's not about money for me."

"Me either." Suddenly, he stole her in the face with all his might.

With a blow to the head, she was immediately unbalanced and surprised at his action. "What...what are you doing?" She slurred, her mouth filling with blood.

He struck her again and again, before smothering her to death with a pillow.

Sweating and panting, when he was done, he tossed the pillow to the floor and looked down at her with bated breath. Easing off of her body, he fell to the floor and vomited by the window.

Bethany Wales, was dead.

Doused in blood, Howard stared down at the freezer. On the floor were the frozen meat packages his mother had given him for sustenance. In its place were pieces of Bet's body, nestled inside. Placing the meat back, he covered her flesh, closed the lid and walked away.

CHAPTER TWENTY-FOUR

The place the Louisville sons rented for Mason, Jersey and Banks in Hawaii was magnificent. The bungalow sat on the water and overlooked a beach so beautiful you could see clear to the bottom. The deck was represented with an infinity pool that spanned the length of the estate. As a result, there wasn't a bad view in sight.

It was as if they were floating on water.

And as Jersey and Mason waded in the pool, Banks sat on the deck glaring at the couple. When he made a decision to cut Jersey off, he never considered having to see her the way she was in the moment. Holding another man, even if it were her husband.

The thing was, he felt in his heart she was doing it on purpose.

Or was she?

Perhaps she really let him go.

The thought of her moving on without him sat on his brain, causing him to think and feel irrational. Did she fuck with his mind the entire time? Was it all a game?

He wasn't sure. So, he was forced to watch as she and Mason flitted around playfully. The look of a happily married couple.

With huge droplets of water splashing about, Jersey would jump on top of him and wrap her legs around his waist as he palmed her ass. Mason may have been living it up, but Jersey was eying Banks, secretly making him pay for breaking her heart.

With Jersey clinging to his body Mason said, "Damn, nigga, you been looking stiff all day. You not getting in the water?"

"No." Banks responded.

"Banks, why you being antisocial?" Jersey said. "After all, we on vacation. You not gonna *break up* the moment are you?"

Catching her play on words, he glared her way.

"Nigga, you good?" Mason asked, confused at his facial expression. "Because you —."

Just at that moment, three women walked along the beach laughing hysterically at one another. Mason, still holding Jersey, yelled, "Ya'll wanna join us?"

Jersey smiled at the ladies, not giving a fuck either which way. "The water's nice up here! Come on up!"

"Ya'll sure?" One of the ladies said.

"Yeah, come on!" Mason said too excitedly, tossing Jersey off his body to make room for more.

At that point Banks had enough. Not feeling like additional company, he got up and walked away as the women joined them in the pool.

The window in Banks' room was open as the moonlight shined inside. He was fast asleep, until the door opened, and Jersey slipped behind him. Her warm body smelling of fresh soap, pressed against his back.

Without looking at her he said, "What you doing here?"

She kissed his ear, her breasts pressed harder against him. "You can't leave me."

"You playing games. I coulda killed you out there tonight. I coulda killed both of you. You don't know me as much as you think you do. Never forget, I murdered my own father."

"I know...I know and I'm so...so sorry, Banks." She kissed the side of his cheek. "But I'm tired of sitting by and not fighting for what I want."

"You could've talked to me. Or are you back with your husband?"

"You broke my heart. And before we started this shit, before we even had sex, you promised never to do that."

He turned on his back and she eased on top of him, before lying her head against his chest. She loved to hear his heartbeat.

"I can't stand to see you with him." He said.

"What does that mean, Banks? Talk to me."

"You know what it means."

"That won't be good enough for me anymore." She looked up at him. "I'm not playing a guessing game. If you want me, if you want my heart, you have to be clearer. And you have to protect it."

"I can't be without you."

"I need to hear the words, Banks."

"It's just me and you."

"What about Mason? Are you gonna change your mind again? If shit gets thick."

"I made a decision to break up not because I'm trying to protect me but because I'm trying to protect you. If he had to choose between me and you, it will be me."

"I know. You said that before. But what do you want?" She said as a single tear snaked down her cheek. "Tell me now you don't want me and I'll go away forever."

"It's me and you against everything." He kissed her lips and her legs spread wider on top of him. "It's me and you against everybody." He pushed into her.

AT THE POOL

After hours, Mason was laughing with the women in the pool when he finally realized Jersey was no longer around. Curious, he grabbed his towel off the edge of the pool and crawled out.

"Where you going?" One of the beauties asked.

"Yeah, we were just having fun," responded another.

"I'm going to find my wife. I be back."

BANKS' ROOM

Banks continued to push into Jersey's pussy. By now she was so wet her juices had meshed into his body and dampened the bed beneath their frames. Their love making was the most passionate he'd ever experienced, and he knew in that moment that nothing would tear them apart.

But death.

BUNGALOW HALLWAY

On the hunt, Mason walked down the hallway leading to Banks' room. He was about to turn the doorknob going into Banks' bedroom, when Banks walked out, wrapped in a white terrycloth robe.

"Why you hiding, nigga?" Mason asked, wobbling a little due to the liquor.

"How you figure I'm hiding?" He fake yawned, praying he wouldn't go into the room and see his wife in his bed. "I thought you and Jersey were having a good time with them females. So I took a nap."

"Nah, Jersey left a little after you."

Banks shrugged. "I guess she figured you were busy too. I swear I think you have a death wish. Cheating on her in her face."

Mason looked into his eyes and wobbled a little. "Did I ever say I was sorry, for, for what happened with me and Bet? On Wales Island. Her pussy wasn't even that good."

"Easy, nigga." He said, although he could give a fuck less about Bet. It was all about Jersey Lou.

"My bad."

Banks readjusted his stance. "Why you bringing that shit up now?"

"I don't know, maybe the alcohol got me going. Whatever the reason, I just wanted you to know." He placed his hand on his shoulder, weighing, heavily.

Banks nodded. "We good now."

"You sure? Because for some reason, sometimes I feel differently."

Banks put his arm around his neck and walked him away from the door. "We good. Let's just live in the moment."

CHAPTER TWENTY-FIVE

D errick and Shay were tucked in bed inside the Lou mansion. The cool air caused them to nestle closely to one another for warmth, which was how both of them preferred to rest. They were in a deep sleep until suddenly Derrick yelled out in pain.

"What the fuck?" He popped up in bed and rubbed his foot, the same one with the amputated toe courtesy of Banks. "Fuck is that?"

She yawned and looked back at him. "What's wrong? Why you yelling and shit?"

Derrick looked at the blood on his fingertips. Slowly he glared at her. "Hold up, you cut me?"

She frowned and turned on the lamp on the side of the bed. "What you talking about?"

He showed her his fingertips. "I'm bleeding. Fuck did you cut me for?"

She eased out of bed, wearing only her panties and bra. "Derrick, why would I do that?" She threw her arms up. "I'm not crazy."

"You sure 'bout that?"

"Hold up, so you really still bringing up that bitch?"

"You mean the girl you killed?"

"That you helped me bury!" She pointed at the window. "Do I gotta remind you 'bout that?"

Silence.

"You know what, I'm not doing this shit with you no more!" She grabbed her robe and stomped toward the exit.

"Where you going?"

"To get something to clean up your fucking blood." She opened the door and stormed out.

Patterson was drinking in the living room while playing a video game when he heard the doorbell ring. Confused, he rose and hit the camera on the surveillance system. When he saw it was Howard, he frowned. There his brother was, posted up at the front door, hands tucked in his coat pockets with fog rolling from his nostrils with each breath.

Curious, he opened the door with the control system and met him in the foyer. "I ain't even know you knew where we lived."

He looked behind him and back at Patterson. "Pops here?"

"Nah, we sent him to Hawaii."

He frowned. "Oh yeah, I...I forgot Derrick told me that." He shuffled a little. "Ya'll...ya'll paid for the trip?"

"Yeah." Something about him seemed jittery and he wondered if he was on drugs. "Why you ask?"

Howard pushed inside and Patterson locked the door. As they moved through the estate, Howard looked around as he was led to the living room. "This nice." Jealousy was laced in his tone. "I see ya'll still doing your thing."

"Yeah, it's cool. Bigger than our other crib."

Howard flopped on the sofa and took off his coat, tossing it to the floor. "Get me a cup of whatever's on the bar."

Patterson poured a glass full of Hennessey, handing it to his brother he poured himself one next. "You gonna tell me why you here? Pops finds out and he'll flip."

He frowned. "Why? He said I can come by if moms here. He just don't wanna see me."

Patterson nodded. "Sooo...why are you here? Ain't like I got a problem with it but..."

"Something happened and I, I mean, I needed my brothers. It's no more and no less."

"You good?" Patterson asked, genuinely concerned. "You need something?"

"Nah, man. I'm not good. But I will be."

"Wanna talk about it?"

"Not now."

Patterson nodded more than he meant to, but the moment was cringey as fuck. "Well, you can stay the night if you want." He took a sip. "I mean, if you not busy."

Howard exhaled in relief, although he tried to hide it afterwards. "Yeah, that...that'll be cool."

THE NEXT DAY

Patterson was lying on the sofa when he smelled an odor. When he woke up, he saw Howard sitting on the sofa looking at TV. Patterson wiped his eyes. "What's that smell?"

"What smell?"

"You don't smell that shit, nigga?" Patterson wiped his eyes again and rushed to the kitchen. Once there, he was shocked to see the backwall over the stove was on fire. Flames were extremely high and reaching toward the ceiling threatening to burn it all. "What the fuck!"

Howard dipped to the sink, turned on the water and began to throw it at the flames. Patterson on the other hand grabbed the fire extinguisher and blasted the fire where it roared.

It took some time but after a while the flames were completely annihilated, leaving dark smoke trails in the air and on the wall.

"Fuck is going on in here?" Derrick asked as he limped inside, due to his foot being cut the night before.

Shay was at his side, coughing.

"This nigga started a fire!" Patterson pointed at Howard.

He frowned. "Me?" He pointed to himself and coughed. "I ain't do this shit!"

"Yeah right!" Patterson coughed. "If you ain't do it, how come when I got up you were sitting up on the sofa looking crazy and shit? It ain't adding up!"

"My nigga, I got some shit on my mind! But I ain't start no fire!"

"What I wanna know is why the smoke detectors didn't go off?" Derrick said.

"He probably turned them off too." Patterson added.

"Why the fuck would I do that?" Howard yelled, throwing his hands up. "I ain't trying to hurt ya'll like this."

"You did it because you an old jealous ass nigga, that's why," Patterson continued. "Mad that pops not checking for you. And now you wanna take it out on us."

"He shouldn't be in here without ma or dad," Derrick said.

Howard stumbled backward. The pain he felt in his chest by hearing his brothers treat him like a stranger, caused him great unease. "So, this how you do your brother?" He looked at them both and waited for an answer. "Ya'll can actually stand here and believe I would do something like this? To my own family."

"Get out, man." Derrick said calmly. "Now."

With his head hung low and his heart broken, he walked out.

"Fuck is your problem?" Derrick said stepping to Patterson. "Why you let that nigga in here when you know he beefing with Pops?"

"Drop it." He coughed again.

"It ain't about dropping it. What we gonna tell Pops when he get back and see this shit all on the wall?"

"I'll have to paint it."

"Yeah, you going to." Derrick said pointing a finger into the center of his chest. "And I ain't putting in on it either. It's coming straight outta your pockets." Derrick and Shay walked away.

CHAPTER TWENTY-SIX

After the maid handed Minnesota her plate of eggs, bacon and toast, she sat across from Tobias in the kitchen who couldn't keep his eyes off of her. "What you looking at?"

He smiled as he scooped some salsa over his meal. "You playing games?"

She giggled. "A girl likes to hear the words."

He looked at the maid and when she left, he sat back. "I love when you don't wear makeup."

"So, I'm ugly with it on?"

"Never said that. It's just that you have natural beauty." He shrugged. "You even seem to glow."

She winked and picked up her phone. When she didn't see what she was looking for she sighed.

"Bad news?" He was concerned for his future wife.

"I been texting my mother all day. Nothing."

"Maybe she has a new friend."

She wished it was true, but she didn't believe it in her heart. "Nah, she still in love with dad. Wouldn't go there with another man."

"Maybe." He said. "But she also knows things aren't going back to the way they used to be." He ate some food. "Maybe she's ready to move on."

"You spoke to, ma?" Spacey asked entering the kitchen.

Minnesota looked at Tobias and back at him. She knew something was up. "I was just telling Tobias I haven't."

"Something's not right." He grabbed a plate and scooped up some bacon and eggs." He sat at the table with them.

"I said the same thing." Minnesota whispered. Now she was very concerned. "I'm just hoping she went out of town to get some alone time." She shrugged. "What you doing here? I thought you were going away with your girlfriend, Joey and his new chick."

"Nah, I was supposed to be having brunch with ma and she didn't hit me back."

Minnesota sat back, having lost her appetite. "Something is really off now. She don't miss no brunch dates for nothing."

Spacey caught the concerned expression in her eyes. He scooped up a few more bites and stood up. "You right." He said chewing with his mouth opened. "I'm going to her apartment. I'll let you know what I find."

The sun spilled over the bungalow in Hawaii effortlessly, as Banks, Mason and Jersey ate breakfast. Although two of them were happy, not everyone was in a good mood.

Wearing a pair of dark shades due to having a hangover, Mason tore into his steak which was prepared by a chef. While Jersey and Banks ate fresh fruit as they laughed and talked about the group of people fighting some ways down on the beach, who were all awful at playing volleyball.

"...he act like it's just her when he's terrible too," Jersey giggled as she peeled off a slice of orange from the shell.

"That nigga going ballistic down there," Banks responded biting a piece of toast. "You'd think this shit was the Superbowl."

"Can ya'll shut the fuck up for five seconds?" Mason yelled. His hangover was so official, it rocked his temples.

Jersey and Banks looked at each other and laughed again.

"Fuck is wrong with you?" Banks asked playfully. "Ain't nobody tell you to take a whole bottle by yourself."

"You ain't lying." Jersey added. "He sent the carriers to get a fresh bottle of Hennessy last night. Crushed the entire thing alone."

Mason looked over at her. "It wasn't just me on that shit."

"I know you not about to act like I tapped it," Banks said pointing at himself. "That was all you."

"He wouldn't be able to remember anyway if he did." Jersey added. "He slept on the beach all night."

"Water almost washed his ass away," Banks responded. "Bitches took his pocket money and all."

As they continued to play with him, something they'd done many times before, Mason grew more and more incensed. Yet they were too high of spirits to notice. Besides, they were in love.

When Banks received a text from Spacey, he read it and frowned.

You heard from ma? She ain't answering her messages.

Banks texted back.

Your mother fine. Don't worry.

"Everything cool?" Jersey asked, seeing the look on his face.

"Yeah, I'm good." He tucked his cell in his pocket.

"Just so ya'll know, me and them fine ass bitches ya'll left me with crushed that bottle together." Mason said dredging up the conversation again. "So ya'll don't know what the fuck you talking about."

His comment was strategic. In the past Jersey would have lit the sky with rage because he was with another woman. But now she simply didn't care.

Banks and Jersey busted out in laughter again.

"Nigga, them females were long gone when you broke that seal," Banks responded.

"I told you he don't remember shit." She giggled a little harder.

Their laughter was like gasoline to his flames. And before long he rose and slapped Jersey across the face with a back hand like a pimp from the 70's.

Silence blanketed the air between them.

And then, things changed.

Enraged, Banks tossed the table over, rushed toward Mason and stole him in the face. The two tussled heavily on the deck, with Banks getting the best of a hungover Mason Louisville.

When Banks was done, he rose and rushed toward Jersey. "You alright?" He asked.

She nodded, while holding her throbbing cheek.

He focused back on Mason. "Me and Jersey flying out tonight."

"Do what you gotta do," Mason responded touching his bloody lip.

Banks and Jersey stormed into the bungalow.

CHAPTER TWENTY-SEVEN

The moon sat over the Louisville estate as Shay showered in Derrick's bathroom. Ever since she did the ultimate, murder, Derrick appeared to be at the very least, interested in the beautiful ticking time bomb.

She was just about to wash her back when the lights went out. It was so pitch black; she couldn't see her hand before her face. "I'm in here, Derrick! Cut the lights back on and shit."

Silence.

"Derrick, turn on the lights! Fuck!" She wiped soap out of her eyes trying to peer into the darkness.

Suddenly the sliding glass door opened, and she was stabbed in her hand. The person attempted to hit her again, but she fought her heart out, until the perpetrator exited, leaving the door open.

Wearing a towel, Shay stormed into the basement with her hand dripping with blood. Derrick and

Patterson were playing Madden until they saw her standing before them with defensive wounds.

Both jumped up.

"Fuck happened to you?" Patterson asked, dropping the controller on the sofa.

Derrick walked up to the bar, grabbed some paper towels and wrapped her hand. "You cut yourself?"

"So, you gonna fake like you don't know what happened?" She asked him.

Derrick frowned. "Hold up, what you trying to say? I did this shit."

"Who else would stab me? I mean, you that mad I killed Jennifer or whatever that chick name was that you would do me like this?"

"Fuck that bitch!"

"Then who stabbed me?"

"I DON'T FUCKING KNOW!" Derrick yelled, using all of his might. Taking a deep breath, he walked away and flopped on the sofa. "MAYBE THE PERSON WHO STABBED MY FOOT!" He calmed down. "Something, something is up."

"You telling me." Patterson said. "Somebody still tossing up my room. Howard's setting fires, your foot getting cut and now Shay's hand."

Derrick looked up at them.

"You think all of this is because of Howard?" Shay asked Derrick. "Like, he doing all of this because he mad at Mason?"

Derrick shrugged. "I don't know. But we need another perspective."

WALES MANSION

Minnesota, Spacey and Tobias stood in the living room, where Patterson, Derrick and Shay were sitting on the sofa. They looked distraught.

"We don't know why he's doing it. Or if he's doing it." Patterson said. "All we know is some strange shit's been happening. And I feel in my heart he behind it."

"I'm not understanding. What you think Howard doing again?" Tobias asked.

"Everything!" Shay said.

"The rooms been getting tossed around," Derrick said. "The other day all of the things in the kitchen cabinet were on the floor."

"The basement had toilet paper thrown everywhere the other night too, remember?" Patterson added.

"Ma's dresses were thrown in the pool earlier," Derrick added.

"Oh yeah, I forgot about that shit," Patterson said.

Slowly Minnesota stepped up to them. "When did this all start happening?"

"I don't know...um, a few days ago." Patterson said.

"But when?" She repeated.

"I can't pinpoint an exact day, right after that shit happened with...you know, the thing we all agreed we wouldn't talk about," Derrick said.

Minnesota frowned. "Let's go back to the house."

LOUISVILLE MANSION

Minnesota, Patterson, Derrick, Spacey, Tobias and Shay stood over the covered hump were Jennifer's body rested in the dirt in the backyard.

"So, all of this strange shit happened right after she died?" Minnesota repeated.

"Yeah, pretty much." Patterson said.

Minnesota smiled and walked toward the house.

"Fuck is she doing?" Derrick asked as they all followed.

"I don't know but it looks like she has an idea." Tobias added.

Before reaching the door, Minnesota said, "When we get inside, don't say a word."

"Why?" Patterson asked.

"Just trust me."

They all entered, and Minnesota quietly walked around every area of the estate. Before long she happened upon the large control room. It was used to hold the central air system.

She smiled and looked back at them.

"I know what's going on." She whispered. "And I know just what to do."

CHAPTER TWENTY-EIGHT

M ason sat on the deck at the bungalow drinking coffee. Once again, he proceeded to outcast the people in his life and he was starting to hate himself for it. He was just about to eat a Danish when one of his workers walked out.

"They flew out earlier today," Nate said. "So, I couldn't give Mrs. Louisville the flowers like you asked. Did you want anything else sir?"

Silence.

"Sir?"

"Get out."

He nodded and walked away.

Taking a deep breath, he dragged a hand down his face just as his phone rang. He started not to answer but luckily for the caller, he wasn't doing anything else in the moment. "What?"

"Wow, you answered."

"What you want, Howard?"

"I wanted...I wanted to apologize. I mean, I realize now that I never got a chance to tell you that. Was too afraid."

Mason chuckled. "You think that solves all?"

"No, I mean, I don't know how much you saw with me and Spacey but—."

"I saw everything."

Howard sighed. "I know now that it was wrong. I know now that being that way is not good. But you should know I'm not gay-gay. I just be fucking around as a joke and shit like that."

"You embarrassed me."

"I know but—."

"There ain't no but. You a man and you took advantage of a nigga who was like a brother to you."

"He could've told me to stop."

"Is that how I raised you?" He paused. "To take what you want anytime you want?"

"Yeah...pretty much."

Mason grabbed his cup of coffee and sipped half down. Suddenly he wished he put a little something brown inside. "I want you to hear me, because what I'm about to say, I won't say again."

"Okay."

"You're dead to me."

"Pops, I'm your son."

"Did you hear me?" He asked, nostrils flaring.

"Yeah, I heard you."

"I'm serious. Ain't no need in you reaching out. Ain't no need in you trying to check my temperature. I will never change on this position. I want nothing else to do with you. If you come to visit your mother, you better make sure I'm not there. If you hanging with Derrick or Pat, you better make sure I'm not around. When I say you're fucking dead to me, that's exactly what I mean."

"But I'm your blood. Your flesh."

"You were. I only have two sons now." With that he ended the call, grabbed the unopened Hennessey bottle sitting across the way and took it to the head.

CHAPTER TWENTY-NINE

Dressed in a robe, Banks hung in the window inside the bedroom of the luxury suite he rented, trying to reach his daughter on the phone. He got back earlier that day from Hawaii and was looking forward to relaxing before dealing with his family and Bolero's package. But Minnesota sounded frantic about not being able to reach Bet and he figured he'd ease her mind. He was certain she was being a brat somewhere and avoiding her family to rattle his nerves. Besides, she told him so the day she hit his car that she would disappear and that he would regret it.

But he couldn't get a hold of Minnesota.

A few minutes later, he walked into the dining room area. Walking up to the table he kissed Jersey on the side of her cheek and sat across from her. The server dished him up eggs, bacon, toast, and a mimosa. "I wanna talk to you about something." He said.

She was smiling until that moment. "Okay, what, what is it this time, Banks?"

"It's over between you and Mason."

She shrugged. "I already know."

"I mean, I don't want you staying in the house. Ever."

She smiled, although she meant to frown. "I haven't been staying there a lot. I stay there about three days a week because I can't...I can't leave the boys. Not right now."

"Jersey, Mason will kill you."

She grabbed her coffee and shook her head. "I wanted to talk to you about that." She took a sip and sat it down. "I mean, you've said it before but I disagree about him murdering me. He's many things but he will never hurt the mother of his children."

"I'm sorry, was I wrong about him punching you repeatedly in the face that one time, with your boys in the house?" He asked sarcastically. "Or smacking you down in Hawaii?"

"You know what I mean."

"What I know is this," he pointed a stiff finger in the table. "If we gonna do, whatever it is we doing, you have to let whatever you have with Mason go." He shrugged. "I mean, ain't that what you wanted?"

"Yes, but I thought we would have more time to —."

"To what, get killed?"

She looked down. "What about you?"

"I can handle myself with Mason. But I've already set up a house in Upper Marlboro for you. They're moving the furniture in as we speak. That way —."

"Banks, if we going to do this, and it's a big if, I don't want you taking care of everything. I want to be involved wherever I live. And however I live."

"And I get all that. But we don't have time. You saw how he treated you in Hawaii. He's a ticking time bomb which means you can't go back home."

She looked down. "But what am I going to tell my sons?" Her voice was barely above a whisper.

"You tell them to look after one another. You tell them to make smarter decisions, and then you let them be men."

"Banks, I'm scared."

He got up and sat next to her. Holding her hand, he said, "I know, and if I thought we had more time, I would transition you out a little easier. But that's not the case."

She nodded knowing he was always the smartest man in the room. "You're right."

He kissed her lips. "You'll be safe. I promise." She took a deep breath and reached under a placemat and handed him a card inside a gold envelope. He frowned. "What's this?"

"Open it."

He flipped it over, pulled off the red plastic seal and pulled out a black card. The front was blank and without words. Inside were two sentences.

I want to have your baby. Will you do me the honor?

He looked at her. "What's this about?"

"It's your birthday."

"How you...how you know? I never talk about it. To anybody."

"I remembered years ago. When you and Mason got back together." She shrugged. "I kept it to memory ever since."

"Wow."

"And I know...I know this is strange but, I had my physical a few weeks ago and I'm healthy. That's one of the reasons I didn't wanna drink. I wanted to be my healthiest self. For you. For your baby."

"So, no drinking was because you..."

"Yes." She kissed him. "So, can I, can I do this for you? Can I do this for us?"

LOU'S MANSION

Spacey, Tobias, Derrick, Patterson and Shay were wearing gas masks inside the Louisville mansion. Each were holding gas cans in their hands and had been given their orders by Minnesota, who was also present.

When it was time to move, she counted to five using her fingers, careful not to make a sound. When all fingers were down, per the plan, each of them ran to various areas within the house, tossing cans in hiding spaces.

A fog like poison rolled everywhere and two minutes later, Sophia came crawling out of a vent, coughing harshly. When she looked up from the floor, she saw the group staring down at her.

"Got you," Minnesota said through her mask.

WAR 5: KARMA

With the house now ventilated, Minnesota, Spacey, Tobias, Derrick, Patterson and Shay stood over Sophia who sat on the basement floor crying in her dingy white bra and panties.

"Are you done?" Minnesota asked not caring about her display of emotions.

She sniffled and wiped her nose with the back of her hand. "Yes."

"Who are you?"

"Sophia Feathers."

"You know what the fuck she means," Patterson snapped.

She exhaled. "That's my name, honestly."

Minnesota walked away and pulled up a chair. Sitting directly in front of her she said, "You can make this hard or easier. It's up to you. But understand this, I won't ask again. Who are you?"

"Sophia is my name and...Nidia sent me."

Everyone gasped, having known the name quite well. Gravely concerned they let the enemy into their home, Derrick stood next to Minnesota. "She sent you here to do what?"

"Kill Banks."

Minnesota was so angry her light skin reddened. "And you planned on doing that how?"

"By getting close to the family and…waiting for the right time." She sniffled again. "But then my sister was killed and, and—."

"You thought you would hide in the house?" Shay yelled, stomping up to her. "And set the kitchen on fire? Stab up people and mess up rooms?" She said throwing her hands around. "That was your fucking stupid ass plan?"

"I wanted, I wanted you to fight with each other and—."

"Bitch, how old are you?" Shay snapped.

"My sister was all I had." She said through clenched teeth. "And I know you all killed her." She looked down. "I have nothing left. So, if you wanna kill me too go ahead. I don't care no more."

CHAPTER THIRTY

After speaking about the future, and what to do with Mason, Banks and Jersey were getting ready for bed when the phone rang. When he saw it was Minnesota, he snatched it quickly. Besides, he'd been trying to get her all day and was unsuccessful. "Where are you? Is everything—."

"Dad, I need you to come to Mason's."

He stood up from the chair. "Mason back in town?"

"No, it's about Nidia. Please hurry."

LOU'S MANSION

Banks sat in the basement alone with Sophia. The others were upstairs, having done their work by isolating the situation and smoking her ass out. Now it was time for him to make a major decision.

Begging for her life with her eyes, her face was still red from having been exposed to gas. "Is it true?" She sniffled.

"Is what true?"

"That you're a woman?"

"Does it matter?" He said.

Silence.

"How would you have done it?" He asked sitting back in his seat as she remained on the floor. "What was your plan, to kill me?"

"I poisoned the punch."

He shook his head. He hated that even after what happened on Wales Island that his family and the Lou's were too lax and allowed in yet another enemy.

"After that I wanted to shoot you." She looked down. "If I had, I wouldn't be in this situation and my sister would be alive."

He chuckled once. "Not much thought into it, huh? If that was the only way you could have done that a long time ago."

"I wanted too." She looked down. "But I think my sister was starting to like Derrick too much."

He nodded, his stare now darker and penetrating.

"So, what you going to do with me?" She looked up at him.

He shrugged and wiped a hand down his face. "What you think I should do?"

She shook her head knowing he was toying with her mind. And it made her hate him even more. "Why the games? If you're going to kill me, let's just get it over with."

"I'm not going to kill you."

"So, it's…it's…torture?" It was her worst fear.

"Nah." He winked. "I'm gonna let you go."

TEXAS AIRPORT

When Sophia exited the plane in Texas, Nidia, flanked by three men, greeted her at baggage claim. She was shocked, scared and relieved to be back home. At the same time, she knew failing to kill Banks didn't do much for her case.

Dropping her luggage, she ran up to Nidia who greeted her with a long hug. With her face nestled in Nidia's bosom, she cried for the loss of her sister. She cried for fearing that Banks would kill her. And most of all, she cried for failing Nidia.

Wiping her tears, she said, "I'm so sorry."

Nidia smiled and with a warm hand to her back said, "Let's go."

An hour later, Nidia and Sophia sat in a restaurant eating savory steak, mashed potatoes and asparagus. Strangely enough, neither said a word, besides, nothing much needed to be said. So much had happened and they both used the moment to sit in peace and silence.

When they both were done, Nidia and Sophia rode in the back of a Mercedes truck, also in silence. Once they arrived at Sophia's house, in a quiet neighborhood in Houston, Nidia said, "I want you to relax," she touched her leg, before dragging the girl's braids over her shoulder. "Things will be fine."

"What does that...what does that mean, Nidia?" She trembled.

"It means that you're good." She smiled. "Everything's good."

"But why?"

She took a deep breath. "I knew Banks would be a lot to handle. And although you both may have been able; it didn't mean you were ready, to complete my mission. Now go home. We'll talk more tomorrow."

Sophia nodded and suddenly her door was opened by Nidia's soldier, he was carrying her luggage. After she exited the vehicle, she took her bag and dragged it on wheels behind her. It was the longest walk of her life. She sensed she would be hit with a bullet from behind with each step and it caused her bladder to weaken although she tried desperately to keep it together.

When she reached her door, she turned around only to see Nidia still sitting in the truck, smiling, sinisterly.

When Sophia smiled, she felt that there was something in the way she looked at her that felt final. That felt...well...over.

Quickly she removed the key from her pocket, unlocked her door and ran inside, leaving her luggage on the porch. Once on the other side of the door she leaned her head on the cool wooden paneling, trying to catch the rhythm of a calm breath. Her braids draped the sides of her face and hung heavy.

When she finished, she turned around and leaned on the door. It was at that time that she saw a stranger in her house. Dressed in all black and a face mask, he was also holding a knife.

"No, no, no, no..." She tried to turn around to exit, but he was already upon her with the knife slowly dragging across her throat.

NIDIA'S ESTATE

Nidia was wrapped in a robe in her bedroom when her special cell phone rang on her bed. She answered. "Yes?"

"We put her up."

She exhaled, having known that Sophia's body was taken away from her home, never to be seen again. With a deep breath she hung up.

Tossing the phone on the bed, she dropped her cell phone and her robe on the floor, preparing to shower.

And then the lights went out.

She frowned.

Because all of the curtains were drawn, her mansion was so dark she couldn't see her hands in front of her face. "Johnson!" She walked around with both hands extended in front of her, hoping not to run into something. "Johnson, what's happening?"

Silence.

"Johnson!"

Fear.

Using her hands even more, she reached around on the floor until she found her robe. And then, she was shoved by someone in the darkness. "Hello...leave me alone!"

Shoved to the floor, her heart rate was so loud it boomed in her ears.

"Who are you?" She yelled. "What do you want with me?"

She was slapped.

"Stop it!" She bumbled around hysterically. "Leave me...leave me alone!"

A harder shove jerked her to the core.

Using all of her might, she rose quickly. Wearing nothing but a bra and panties set, she ran down the steps, slipping and sliding everywhere due to sweaty feet. But she had to hurry because she felt someone behind her, ready to do her harm.

Once in her foyer, she was pushed again from behind as she tried to make it to the door. "Please, please stop! Leave me, leave me alone!"

Bare feet slapping against the floor, she rushed toward the back door trying to get some light. Screaming for help was out of the question because her estate sat on acres, surrounded by woods and away from civilization.

Pulling the sliding glass door open, she stumbled onto the grass and flipped on the light. And there, under the night sky was the Wales and Lou gang. Including, Banks, Mason, Spacey, Derrick, Patterson, Tobias, Minnesota and Shay.

All were dressed in black.

All were looking in her direction.

All had been waiting.

Turning her head, she saw a large man she didn't know, the man who was pushing her around inside. And when she squinted, in the distance she saw the new Wales aircraft, and wondered why she hadn't heard it flying above.

Shaking her head, she took a deep breath. "Do you really think you can kill me, Banks? Do you really not understand what would happen to you? And how many families would go unfed? You wouldn't last a day after they hunted you down!"

Silence.

"Do you really not know who I am? And what I'm capable of?" She continued. "My men are in my house and they will kill each and every one of you." She pointed at the sliding glass door. "Run now, all of you, while you still can!"

Derrick, Spacey, Patterson and Tobias raised their hands, each were holding the heads of her men. And it was at that time that she also saw the machetes in their grasps.

Minnesota walked up to her slowly and slapped her face. "That's for what you put my family through, all these years."

Nidia smiled, although her heart rocked inside. "I see myself in you. And you will have a hard life."

Banks approached seconds later, standing at her side. Looking down at Nidia he said, "I should've killed you when I had the chance."

Her heart rocked.

"I won't make that mistake again." Banks and Minnesota backed away, and just like that, she was lit up with gunfire.

CHAPTER THIRTY-ONE

Mason chased Jersey around the bedroom as she yanked her clothing from drawers and closets. "We've fought before, Jersey!" He threw his arms up. "So, I hit you when I was drunk? So what! Don't leave me like this!"

"I can't do this with you anymore." She tossed a pile of clothing into her suitcase.

"Just because I made a mistake?"

She dropped the bundle of clothing she was holding on the bed. It was obvious that he was trying to rouse anger in her, so that she'd say something. She knew she should just leave, but she couldn't resist responding.

"A mistake? Is that what you call fucking your best friend's wife? Mason, you destroyed what we built. What I was trying to create with you. And I can't anymore with you."

"Yes." He looked down. "I, I was messed up. We just lost Arlyndo and —."

"Don't do that." She pointed in his face. "You don't get the right to bring up my son's name like that."

"He was my son too."

"And look how you treat his legacy. What are you doing differently? Since he died. You still the same drunk you were when I met you. And I want more. I want a love story. I want happiness. I want a life."

"And where you gonna get that?" He threw up his arms. "Because keep it one hundred, who makes more money than me? Who can afford to take you around the world? Huh?"

"Your mindset is so small."

"Nothing about me is small."

"Yes, it is. You think everything can be explained away in dollars and cents. Well I don't give a fuck about money anymore. I want…I want more."

He lowered his brow. "Without money you'll have every struggle in the world."

"Without love, Mason. You have nothing without love."

He took a deep breath. "Okay, you won!"

She leaned her head back. "What you talking about now?"

"We can do counselling."

She busted into heavy laughter.

"Fuck is funny?"

"We way past counselling. I mean think about it, what are we going to do, tell people about the murders and the drugs? Because when you think about how we got here, you have to talk about everything. Are you willing to talk about *everything*?"

"Stop being stupid."

"That's what I'm saying. Look how you talk to me. You don't respect me." She paused. "You never have. Whenever the conversation gets thick, you want to shut me up. You want to shut me down. No more."

He looked away. "Where will you go?"

She started packing again. "I don't know."

"For a woman who doesn't know, you're sure moving quickly."

She zipped the bag and dragged it off the bed. "I'm sorry. But I'm done." She walked out of the room and right into Derrick who was standing in the hallway.

"So, you really gonna do this?" He whispered.

"What you talking about, Derrick?"

"I know, ma. I been knew."

She looked behind her at the bedroom door. Mason had closed it. Feeling more comfortable she whispered, "I didn't want this to happen. I loved your father. I still do...but...I mean..."

"Why, ma? I mean, Banks is his best friend. Why you wanna rip him up like this?"

"So, I shouldn't be happy?"

"It's not about being happy. You and Lil Fizz can't run off and be together just 'cause you mad at how Pops moved in the past. With Aunt Bet. You wrong this time, ma."

She took a deep breath. "I raised my sons into men. Even though, even though sometimes you made decisions that made me sad. It didn't matter. I still accepted you. Now you have to accept me."

"Ma, don't do this."

"No listen. Finally, for the first time in my life I'm gonna be selfish. And I'm sorry if you can't understand that. I really am." She stood on her toes and kissed him on the cheek before walking away.

LOU'S MANSION - BACKYARD

Patterson yawned as he dragged the trash can to the enclosed unit in the back of the house. When he saw his brother, he stopped in his tracks. Howard's eyes were wide, glassed over and strange.

"What you doing out here? And how you get over the gate?"

Silence.

In that moment, Patterson thought about how he treated Howard, for blaming him for things Sophia did and took a deep breath. "Listen, man, I'm sorry 'bout the kitchen thing. With the fire and all. Turns out we had this female hiding in the house and—."

"I would've never done anything to hurt you," He looked like a maniac. "It's like everybody but ma ain't got no problem turning they back on me. Why is that? Ain't my last name Louisville too?"

"I know shit fucked up but it's not like we don't fuck with you. I mean, I wish I knew what really went on with you and Pops." He walked up to him and placed a hand on his shoulder. "But everything will be fine. I'ma talk to Pops later today. You just have to—."

A knife to the gut cut-off his statement.

Patterson's eyes flew open as he released the hold on his brother's shoulder. Wounded, Patterson fell to the ground and Howard lowered his height and climbed on top of him. Looking quickly at the sliding glass door, he covered his mouth and stabbed him several more times in the gut.

When he closed his eyes, Howard backed off of him, covered in his brother's blood.

"I'm sorry," he uttered, before crying and running away.

Howard drove frantically down the street while making a call. "I thought I told you not to hit my number." Mason said calmly.

"You said you have other sons." Howard yelled as tears rolled down his face. "Is that what you said to me, nigga?"

"WHAT YOU WANT?" Mason roared, not in the mood for games.

"I want you to know one thing. You did this. Not me!"

"You got five seconds to tell me what you're talking about. Four of 'em are gone already."

"Okay then let me say this, you one more son short, my nigga and I have one more to go!" He tossed the phone in the passenger seat and sped faster down the freeway.

WAR 5: KARMA

CHAPTER THIRTY-TWO

The room was crowded as they waited on the news in the hospital. Did Patterson survive a terrible act perpetrated on him by his own brother? No one knew for sure, but it didn't look good.

Mason was devastated. It was less than a year and already he was faced with burying another son. Luckily, the support team was on deck. Just like in the past, all of the Wales' and Lou's were bounded by an overwhelming moment, with the exception of Joey and of course, Howard.

After all, why would he be there? Because of his jealousy, because of the malice he held in his heart, he decided to smite his own brother.

Feeling like the world was spinning, Mason sat in his chair, staring down at the patterns on the cream tile floor. For the second it appeared that he was still a married man, as Jersey was to his right, holding his hand. Banks was propped up in the chair on his left and kept a warm hand to Mason's back.

"This can't be happening," Mason whispered.

Banks looked over at Jersey whose eyes were so red, you could barely see the white surfaces underneath. Unlike in the past, she didn't look at him, her gaze remained down, distraught and afraid. He wanted to hold her, but it would be gravely inappropriate.

Across the room Minnesota rested in Tobias' arms as they leaned against the wall. Near, Shay sat on Derrick's lap, doing her best to ease his pain with soft strokes on the back. While Spacey leaned against the wall alone. He himself knew what Howard was capable of, but still, he never expected this.

After what seemed like forever, finally a doctor walked up to the family and his eyes said everything they needed to know.

Patterson Louisville was dead.

HOWARD'S APARTMENT

Flanked by three men, Mason and Banks kicked through Howard's apartment door. When they got inside, they were surprised to see the house so neat, with everything in place. It was shocking since he just ruined everyone's life.

Patterson was dead. And still he had time to clean?

Mason's nostrils flared as he stormed through the house, pushing things over, with Banks at his side. "Where is he?" Mason whispered, eyes as red as apples. "Fuck is he?"

"I don't know, man, but we gonna find him." Banks took a deep breath. "Let's keep looking. Maybe we'll find a clue."

Banks entered the living room and then the den. It was as if they were on a futile scavenger hunt. After fifteen minutes of searching, he found nothing that would bring them closer to Howard. And then he moved to the kitchen, mostly to be thorough than anything else.

After searching on the top of the fridge and inside the cabinets, for some reason Banks opened the deep freezer. What he saw next didn't make sense. At first glance, his mind saw frozen steaks, hot dogs and such. But when he blinked a few more times, he saw his ex-wife's head inside, eyes open as if looking at him.

Stunned, he backed up and slammed into the wall, before sliding down. His soldiers were at his side.

"Boss, you good?" One asked. "You...you need anything?"

Hearing the noise Mason ran inside and when he saw the freezer, he was shocked. Surely things couldn't have gotten worse. Surely, they suffered enough for their past aggressions.

Did they deserve more pain?

Apparently, the answer was yes, because Banks would have to tell his family the ultimate. That their mother was gone.

Banks walked into the living room of his estate, where Minnesota, Joey and Spacey sat on the sofa. The second they saw his face, Minnesota dropped to her knees and Banks ran over to catch her.

Words didn't need to be said in that moment.

It was obvious that Bethany Wales was gone and once again their life would never return to normal.

"I'm going to make him pay for this," Banks said as he held his crying daughter. "I p

romise."

BETHANY WALES FUNERAL

It had been a long day. The longest in Banks' life. Never had he experienced so many emotions in a matter of months. First, he almost lost his daughter, only to have her returned. Then he lost his son only to later have his island taken over by his wife's crazy ex-boyfriend. Then Arlyndo died and a little while after that he experienced real love at the hands of his best friend's wife.

With everything swirling in his heart, he feared a breakdown nearing.

As Mason and Banks attended the second funeral of the week, that of Bethany Wales, Banks couldn't deal with the sound of her parents crying. They always felt he would be the cause of her death and they were right. His kids, Minnesota, Spacey and Joey were in a state too.

"What you gonna do about Howard?" Banks said, as the preacher spoke to the congregation.

"Nothing. He my son."

Banks looked at him. "He killed Pat and Bet. He can't—."

"I know but I...I...I should've handled him a different way."

Banks nodded, although he didn't agree. "What did he do? To cause you to cut him off?"

Mason looked into his eyes. "I tell you everything. You know I do. But this...this I gotta take with me. To my grave."

"Why?"

Mason looked at Spacey who's head was lowered to prevent looking at his mother's casket. "Because I made a promise. Sorry, man, but I gotta leave it at that."

Banks sat back and dragged his sweaty hands down his pants. His eyes settled on Jersey, who hadn't looked at him since she lost her son. He wasn't even sure if they were still together. But his heart said no, and he felt selfish even thinking about it.

"You think this our fault?" Mason said, softly.

Banks sighed and fell back into the bench, emotionally exhausted and bent. "Why you ask that?"

"Whenever we got good shit happening, a little while later, the bad comes. Fuck is the problem?"

"I don't..." he took a deep breath. "I don't know, Mason. I mean, we deal in a product that fucks up people's lives. And…and I know that…so…maybe the life span for niggas like us is short anyway."

Mason looked at the casket. "And those we love too."

"So, if you asking, I'll say yes, maybe this is karma."

Bolero waited patiently in an office he rented for the business meeting with Banks. Two minutes earlier than the scheduled time, Banks walked inside with Minnesota, Shay, Joey, Spacey and Tobias.

Tobias and Spacey were holding two duffle bags of cash each.

"You're on time." Bolero said.

"Why wouldn't I be?" Banks asked.

"It's just that with everything that's been happening in your family. I figured — ."

"My mother's death has nothing to do with this," Minnesota snapped, ready to kill at will.

Mr. Bolero smiled. He'd seen enough to know that this young lady was changing. She was beautiful. Young. And smart. At the end of the day she had the world ahead of her. Which wasn't necessarily a good thing, especially if she had criminal intentions in mind.

"So, do you have something for me?" Mr. Bolero asked, wanting to get to the heart of the matter.

Banks looked back and Tobias and Spacey brought the bags forward, sitting them on the table. Bolero's men went through each bag and nodded to Bolero after every stack was tested and accounted for.

"Well, it looks like our business relationship has concluded." Bolero said. "All of my money is here. The debt is paid. And I'm sure my client will be happy."

"I know there's no client." Banks said calmly. "There never was."

Bolero frowned. "What do you mean?"

"It took me some time, but I knew I recognized your face." He shuffled a little. "It's funny. Even when I try to fall back, even when I try not to be so, so critical, I still see shit other people don't."

"Has to be a hard life. Not to be able to trust."

"I'm in the business of being sure." Banks responded. "Trust is never an option. Anyway, after a while, I knew where I saw you. It was from an article dated some years back. I was doing research for Wales island before I bought it and your face came up as the person who owned the property. On the front of the property was a sign meant to spark fear in those who didn't fall in line." And in what sounded like pitch perfect Spanish, he said, "*Con el tiempo serás un recuerdo.*"

Bolero smiled and translated. "In time, you will be a memory."

"So I researched a little further over the past few days. And found out you ran a cartel called *Los Esqueletos*. If your money was short a dollar, you had them killed, their bodies never found. In fact, Wales Island was built on skulls. The men and women who died due to your war. Which was why you called it Skull Island."

Bolero sat back.

"You were the mastermind, but it was your brother who took the fall and got sentenced for your crimes." He paused. "And the Nunez girls, who died on my island, are your children." He looked back at Tobias. "He is too."

Tobias frowned.

Bolero smiled. "Even if that were true why would I tell you?"

"But is it true?" Tobias asked really wanting to know. He'd known the man for a long time, but never in a personal situation.

"The only truth you need to worry about is that you've found happiness. Be grateful."

Tobias glared.

"What I never got was why?" Banks continued. "Why keep your kids in poverty? Why put them in a situation where they worked for me as maids?" He continued. "Why…"

Suddenly Banks understood everything.

"You knew the person who purchased Wales Island would be a dealer. And you used the property as bait, knowing someone like me would come along, and you could get put back on."

"Is it true?" Tobias said louder. "I mean, tell me something."

Bolero clasped his fingers together on the desk and sat back. "You've fulfilled your end of the bargain, Banks. There's nothing else to talk about now."

"We want another pack." Banks said plainly.

Bolero frowned. "I'm confused. You made yourself perfectly clear that you wanted out of the business."

"And you knew that would be a lie. You knew once the flood gates opened, that we would need to keep the product coming. For ourselves. For our soldiers and for your greed. Because if we walk away, it will be *Con el tiempo serás un recuerdo* for us too." In other words. "If we leave, you'll have us killed. This was always a trap."

Bolero grinned. "Even if I wanted to work with you again, why should I trust you? I mean, you did attempt to call me out just now."

"You're a businessman, right?"

"I am."

"So, there's your answer. I mean, when it comes to moving weight, nobody is better. We are still useful to you. There's no reason to execute myself and my family."

"You should think long and hard about getting into business with me. This isn't something I take lightly. You don't pay and everybody who ever whispered your name will die."

"We ready to work." Banks glared. "The only question is, do you prefer us dead or alive?"

CHAPTER THIRTY-THREE

Jersey walked up to Mason's mansion after getting a call from Derrick that his father wasn't doing well. The moment she reached the circular driveway she saw Mason sitting in his truck with no shirt on. She opened the passenger's door and trembled when she saw a gun sitting on his towel wrapped lap.

He looked at her and smiled. "Get in."

"Mason, what's —."

"Get in!"

Slowly she complied, pressing her back against the door in case she had to escape. "What's going on?"

"I wanna tell you..." He choked up. "To tell you I'm sorry for everything."

"Mason, it's not your fault what Howard did." Her heart broke at the thought of losing a son again. "That's on him. I mean, you know that right? He will be fine. I feel it in my heart."

He didn't.

"I isolated him. Pushed him away when, when all he wanted was to talk."

"Why?"

He exhaled. "I walked in on him raping Spacey."

WAR 5: KARMA

Her eyes flew open in disbelief. "What...what you talking about raping Spacey?"

"It was on the island. In the sauna. And I...I guess it reminded me about what I'd been through as a kid."

He never wanted to talk about those moments. And suddenly she was more interested. "I don't...I don't understand." She felt dizzy. "And what you go through? Talk to me!"

He looked down, unwilling to speak on the rape by his uncle. "It doesn't matter. I should've, I guess I should've helped him when he needed me the most."

Now everything made sense, although things were still so hard to process. She felt breathless. "Does Banks know?"

"I can never tell him. Especially now."

She looked at the weapon in his lap. "Mason, what are you about to do?"

He picked the gun up and put it to his head.

Mason was lying in a hospital bed inside Jerry's Mental Institution. When he woke out of his drug induced state, and turned his head, Banks was sitting in the chair waiting. "How long I been out?"

"This time?"

He frowned. "I woke up before?"

"Yeah, man. You been here for two weeks. And every time you ask me the same thing."

Mason was stunned. "You gonna take me home?"

"They admitted you. They think you still a danger to yourself. I think it's a good thing you're here too. For the rest."

"How's Jersey?"

"She's shaken up." Banks shifted a little. "Never had to wrestle a gun from your hand before. Never wants to again. You blacked her eye in the fight. She's…she's scared."

He knew their marriage was over now. Too much happened. "I know I scared her. I'm gonna make it up to her when—."

"Don't, man." He waved the air.

"Don't what? Fight for my wife?"

"Don't think about anything but getting better." Banks' statement was more of a demand than a request. If he had it his way, he'd never see her again.

Mason nodded. "How long you been here? Been coming?"

"Every day," he said truthfully before taking a deep breath. "It's the first place I come before doing anything else. I have to run some errands now though. But I'll be back tomorrow." He rose and shook his hand.

Banks was almost to the door when, "Banks."

He turned to face him.

"What God has joined together let no man tear apart, without first catching a bullet."

Banks smiled at hearing the quote they used to share as young men. Although now, the words felt ominous and more like a premonition of things to come. "You know, I always thought that quote was fit more for a married couple then friends."

Mason stared at him intensely. "Maybe you're right."

Banks walked into the Lou's mansion. The cleaning crew he hired was still inside because Jersey hadn't been back in over a month but had been sending meals. When he walked to the foyer he was greeted by Shay.

"How's Derrick?"

She shrugged. "Bad." Truth was he was breaking down having lost two brothers and it was easy to understand why.

"How are you?" He asked.

"Maintaining." She hugged him. "Please thank Jersey for meal prepping for us. He hasn't eaten much but I have. I need the energy to take care of him. You heard from Jersey?"

He nodded.

"Is she good?"

"She's dealing."

"You want to see Derrick?" She continued.

"Nah." He kissed her cheek. "I have some place to go. But I'll check on you both later next week."

"Thank you, dad."

He nodded and walked out.

Howard had his fill of alcohol for the evening, as he strolled into The Viking club. Sitting in the lounge area, barely able to hold up a seat, he was preparing to call over two men when suddenly the manager approached.

"You have to leave." His hands were clasped in front of him, and he had a bodyguard on the right and left.

Howard frowned, his words slurring. "Leave for what? I'm a…a paying…paying customer."

"Don't make me say it again."

Looking at the body-built men at his side, Howard rose and traipsed out. He had planned on getting satisfied by a few good men and women, so being dismissed from his favorite spot put him in a dark mood. Unwilling to go home, fifteen minutes later, he was in an alley getting his dick sucked by a stranger. It didn't take him long to reach an orgasm, so he was in his motel room twenty minutes after that.

After showering, he dried off, lotioned up and got in bed. Alone inside his dark motel room, visions of what he'd done to his brother played in his mind. The worst part of it all was simple. If Patterson was alive, and he had it to do all over again, he would kill him.

Thinking he was hearing things, he rolled over to his side when he heard the door open. Curious, he sat up in bed quickly when he saw Banks enter with three men.

The moment Howard motioned to turn on the light, one of Banks' men rushed to his side, stealing him in the face.

Slowly, and with all the time in the world, Banks strolled deeper inside the room and sat on the bed. It squeaked.

"How'd you find me?" Howard trembled.

"I always knew where you were."

His eyes widened. "So, so, you gonna kill me?"

Banks nodded. "Yes."

Howard's blood ran cold. "Please don't. I...I made a mistake and I...my life was messed up. My, my father ignored me. He, he abandoned me. But if I had it to do all over again, I wouldn't kill my brother. I wouldn't have killed Bet either. I loved —."

"There's no need in crying. My mind is made up. I just wanna know why?"

He wept quietly. "I don't wanna —."

"WHY DID YOU KILL BET!?"

Howard exhaled. "Because she was going to tell on you. About what you were doing with my mother."

The moment he heard the words he realized it didn't matter. They were weak, fruitless and too dumb a reason to take a life. As he sat on the bed, looking at him through the dark, he could tell Howard was void of emotion. The man was damaged, and he was sure by killing him he'd be doing the world a favor.

Plus, with his death, his secret relationship with Jersey would go with him.

"Do it," he responded.

And on his word, the men strangled him to death. And they all walked out of the room.

Mason and Banks were watching television at the mental institution. When the commercial came on Banks said, "I'll be gone for a little while. I have to take care of some things, for myself."

Mason frowned and readjusted in bed. "Gone...gone where?"

"I need a break, man. From everything."

Mason looked down and back at the television. "I heard you reupped the package."

Banks nodded. "We did."

"I thought you wanted out?" Mason readjusted the hospital band on his arm.

"It was always a trap, man. We were never supposed to leave. And with Bolero being worse than Nidia, this is our new life. Gotta get used to it."

Mason nodded. "Anybody heard from Howard?"

"Not since I told you he was spotted in Miami." He shrugged. "I think you should give up on finding him though. He knows he's done too much. Let it go."

"Maybe you're right."

Banks stood up and touched his covered leg. "Later, Mason."

Mason looked at him for what felt like forever. "Later."

CHAPTER THIRTY-FOUR
UPPER MARLBORO, MD

The midwives fussed around Jersey as she lied in a bed within the maternity room Banks had set up for her on her estate. He was proud as he looked down at the woman who had just given birth to his twin boys which they named Ace and Walid.

They were his flesh and blood.

When they were done cleaning her and the babies, Banks sat on the side of the bed and looked down at the nude infants she nestled against her body. He pulled the covers up enough to give all three warmth.

Smiling proudly, he wiped her hair behind her ear and looked down at her beautiful face. "You, you actually did it."

"What?" She said, already knowing the answer but loving to hear the words. The babies cooed lightly.

"You gave birth to twins."

"Your sons." She emphasized. "Of your flesh and blood."

He nodded, more proudly.

When Jersey first said she wanted to give him babies, he thought she was lying. After all, she would have to go through the invasive process of having Banks' eggs implanted with a sperm donor and deposited into her body. The same thing Bet did with Minnie.

Originally the procedure netted in quintuplets, but he later had three removed to allow for an easier pregnancy. It was an invasive procedure, but she was game for it, in the name of love.

"I've never been happier." He admitted.

"And I'm so pleased I could do this for you, Banks." She looked up at him and smiled.

"I'm happy for you too."

When Banks heard another voice in the room, chills ran down his spine when he turned around, to see Mason hanging in the doorway.

Smiling.

Trying to get him away from the love of his life and his twins he quickly rose and said, "Let's talk out there."

"Nah," he walked deeper into the room. "We talking right here."

It was at that time Banks could see the five men in the hallway, holding the midwives and two of his bodyguards at gunpoint.

As if they knew what was coming, both babies suddenly wept.

"Mason, please, please don't," Jersey whispered as tears trailed her cheek and fell on her babies faces.

"Don't do what? Allow you to live in peace and harmony with my best fucking friend? You gave this nigga babies!" He roared. "It's one thing to fuck her," he said looking at Banks. "But, ya'll niggas crossed the line." He put his hands on his chest. "I mean, is it just me or are ya'll actually in LOVE?!" Tears rolled down his cheeks.

"Mason, it's not like you didn't — ."

"I'M NOT TRYING TO HEAR THAT SHIT ABOUT ME FUCKING BET NO MORE!" He said, cutting Jersey off. "THE GUILT TRIP SHIT IS DEAD! IT WAS DONE WHEN IT WAS DONE!" He took a deep breath. "But you two, you two took it too far. You fell in love."

She looked at Banks who shuffled a few steps. "What you want, Mason? Anything you want and it's done." Banks wasn't a begging man. But he would get on his knees if he thought it was worth it. Besides, he just met his sons and already he was deeply in love with them. And he would do what was necessary to protect their newborn lives.

"I want to tell you something that's very important." Mason smiled. "Something you may wanna know."

Banks glared, not trusting his disposition or motives. "What?"

"I found out early on about all this baby making shit. I just wanted, I just wanted you to tell me yourself, nigga. That last time you visited me in the institution." Mason continued, trembling with rage. "You owed me more but you, you couldn't do it. And I remember thinking, I can't believe my guy is this foul."

Jersey said, "Mason, can we talk about—"

"You don't say shit else to me," he responded, aiming his barrel at Jersey's head. "I'm done with yo ho ass!"

Banks stepped in front of the gun, blocking the barrel's path.

Unable to kill his man, Mason lowered it and looked down. "I knew before she did the procedure. Had her followed when she left the house."

"How?" Banks asked.

"Derrick told me." He walked away. "So I, so I let her do it. I let her have your babies. But you need to know something, Banks. Those kids, those boys, are *ours*."

Banks frowned and stepped back. "What...what...you...what you talking about?"

"I don't need to tell you that with money you can do anything. So, it was easy to have my sperm mixed with your eggs for this procedure." He smiled like a mad man and walked over to Jersey. Looking down at their twins he said, "I mean, look what we built. They're perfect."

Jersey's eyes widened as she stared down at the babies, trying to find one hint of it being true. And there, on Ace's hand, was a tiny birthmark that Howard also had on his little finger. And she knew it was all facts.

Banks backed into the wall and slid down.

"We created a new generation of Lou's and Wales'." He walked over to Banks and stood over top of him. "And it's perfect. Don't you see, Banks. Ain't no getting rid of me. Ain't no getting rid of us now."

"I...I can't believe...you...did this." Banks whispered.

"What God has joined together let no man tear apart, without first catching a bullet." Mason smiled. "We joined together now. Which brings me to my next question. You have one decision to make. Just one." He put his hand over his heart.

Banks eyes were glassed over and red, having been exposed to his betrayal of the highest order. Mason had been wanting them to be combined all his life, and finally he created a situation where they had children together.

Two beautiful twin boys.

"What...what do you want?" Banks glared.

"You have to choose. Do you want our sons or Jersey's life?" He stooped down. "Because you can't have both. So, tell me my love, what's it gonna be?"

CARTEL PUBLICATIONS

PRESENTS

The Cartel Publications Order Form

www.thecartelpublications.com

Inmates **ONLY** receive novels for $10.00 per book **PLUS** shipping fee **PER BOOK.**

(Mail Order **MUST** come from inmate directly to receive discount)

Shyt List 1	_____	$15.00
Shyt List 2	_____	$15.00
Shyt List 3	_____	$15.00
Shyt List 4	_____	$15.00
Shyt List 5	_____	$15.00
Pitbulls In A Skirt	_____	$15.00
Pitbulls In A Skirt 2	_____	$15.00
Pitbulls In A Skirt 3	_____	$15.00
Pitbulls In A Skirt 4	_____	$15.00
Pitbulls In A Skirt 5	_____	$15.00
Victoria's Secret	_____	$15.00
Poison 1	_____	$15.00
Poison 2	_____	$15.00
Hell Razor Honeys	_____	$15.00
Hell Razor Honeys 2	_____	$15.00
A Hustler's Son	_____	$15.00
A Hustler's Son 2	_____	$15.00
Black and Ugly	_____	$15.00
Black and Ugly As Ever	_____	$15.00
Ms Wayne & The Queens of DC **(LGBT)**	_____	$15.00
Black And The Ugliest	_____	$15.00
Year Of The Crackmom	_____	$15.00
Deadheads	_____	$15.00
The Face That Launched A Thousand Bullets	_____	$15.00
The Unusual Suspects	_____	$15.00
Paid In Blood	_____	$15.00
Raunchy	_____	$15.00
Raunchy 2	_____	$15.00
Raunchy 3	_____	$15.00
Mad Maxxx (4th Book Raunchy Series)	_____	$15.00
Quita's Dayscare Center	_____	$15.00
Quita's Dayscare Center 2	_____	$15.00
Pretty Kings	_____	$15.00
Pretty Kings 2	_____	$15.00
Pretty Kings 3	_____	$15.00
Pretty Kings 4	_____	$15.00
Silence Of The Nine	_____	$15.00
Silence Of The Nine 2	_____	$15.00
Silence Of The Nine 3	_____	$15.00
Prison Throne	_____	$15.00

By T. STYLES 273

Drunk & Hot Girls	_____	$15.00
Hersband Material **(LGBT)**	_____	$15.00
The End: How To Write A	_____	$15.00
Bestselling Novel In 30 Days (Non-Fiction Guide)		
Upscale Kittens	_____	$15.00
Wake & Bake Boys	_____	$15.00
Young & Dumb	_____	$15.00
Young & Dumb 2: Vyce's Getback	_____	$15.00
Tranny 911 **(LGBT)**	_____	$15.00
Tranny 911: Dixie's Rise **(LGBT)**	_____	$15.00
First Comes Love, Then Comes Murder	_____	$15.00
Luxury Tax	_____	$15.00
The Lying King	_____	$15.00
Crazy Kind Of Love	_____	$15.00
Goon	_____	$15.00
And They Call Me God	_____	$15.00
The Ungrateful Bastards	_____	$15.00
Lipstick Dom **(LGBT)**	_____	$15.00
A School of Dolls **(LGBT)**	_____	$15.00
Hoetic Justice	_____	$15.00
KALI: Raunchy Relived	_____	$15.00
(5th Book in Raunchy Series)		
Skeezers	_____	$15.00
Skeezers 2	_____	$15.00
You Kissed Me, Now I Own You	_____	$15.00
Nefarious	_____	$15.00
Redbone 3: The Rise of The Fold	_____	$15.00
The Fold (4th Redbone Book)	_____	$15.00
Clown Niggas	_____	$15.00
The One You Shouldn't Trust	_____	$15.00
The WHORE The Wind		
Blew My Way	_____	$15.00
She Brings The Worst Kind	_____	$15.00
The House That Crack Built	_____	$15.00
The House That Crack Built 2	_____	$15.00
The House That Crack Built 3	_____	$15.00
The House That Crack Built 4	_____	$15.00
Level Up **(LGBT)**	_____	$15.00
Villains: It's Savage Season	_____	$15.00
Gay For My Bae	_____	$15.00
War	_____	$15.00
War 2: All Hell Breaks Loose	_____	$15.00
War 3: The Land Of The Lou's	_____	$15.00
War 4: Skull Island	_____	$15.00
War 5: Karma	_____	$15.00

(**Redbone 1** & **2** are **NOT** Cartel Publications novels and if **ordered** the cost is **FULL** price of $15.00 **each**. **No Exceptions**.)

Please add **$5.00** for shipping and handling fees for up to **(2) BOOKS PER ORDER**.

Inmates too!

(See Next Page for ORDER DETAILS)

WAR 5: KARMA

The Cartel Publications * P.O. BOX 486 OWINGS MILLS MD 21117

Name: _____

Address: _____

City/State: _____

Contact/Email: _____

*Please allow **8-10 BUSINESS** days **Before** shipping.*

The Cartel Publications is _NOT_ responsible for _Prison Orders_ rejected!

NO RETURNS and NO REFUNDS
NO PERSONAL CHECKS ACCEPTED
STAMPS NO LONGER ACCEPTED

By T. STYLES   275